DISCARD

# the girl on the dock

*A Petra Morganstern Story Written and Illustrated by*

## G. Norman Lippert

# *The Story of the Story*

Greetings, dear reader, and welcome to "The Girl on the Dock". Before you begin the tale, I thought it might be rather helpful for me to tell you the story of the story.

A little over a year ago, I embarked upon a writing project. It was meant to be just for fun, for my own enjoyment and that of a few family and friends. The project was a cathartic exercise, following the story of a certain well known young wizard—not quite as famous as his father (thus forming the nature of this young wizard's primary problem) but famous nonetheless. To my surprise, this writing project grew into a full length novel. On a lark, I released the novel online. There, amazingly, it achieved a rather shocking worldwide readership. This led, of course, to a sequel.

With the release of the sequel, I discovered a few interesting things: while based in the essential storyline of another famous author (thus forming the nature of some of my own ticklish problems) these stories had come to encompass an awful lot of original concepts and characters. I realized with some degree of delight that there was an entirely new storyline embedded there, and that it was unique to me.

Thus, I embarked on a new writing project: I broke away from the trunk of the original idea and I transplanted some of my own unique branches into a new story. This, dear reader, is the result of that experiment.

So what does this mean to you? Well, there are two ways you may choose to enjoy this story:

First, since this tale is, in many ways, a logical progression from my first two novels, you may choose to read those first. They can be found free online, beginning with www.elderscrossing.com. There, you will find the back story of the characters contained herein, which will surely allow you to appreciate this tale on a somewhat broader scale.

Second, you may choose to launch into this story as its own entity. It was written to stand alone, even if much of the back story exists elsewhere. The struggles and concepts that form the core of this story, while fantastic and magical (and rather dark) will be familiar to most readers, even if they've never read the names of these characters before. If you choose to read the story on its own, it will be helpful (though not necessary) for you to be aware of a few things: first, our main character, the teenaged Miss Morganstern, is a member of a secret magical society that exists alongside the non-magical world. Second, she has had a rather unusual last year of schooling, during which she was the center of a rather shocking plot by some very bent wizards. The details of that plot will become known as the following story progresses, but the essential result of that plot was this: Miss Morganstern has discovered that she is cursed with the final, fragmented ghost of the most evil wizard of all time. Like a flame in a lantern, this wicked shred of soul lives inside her own soul, affecting her, influencing her. In this, Petra is not unlike all of us, cursed as we are with the dual nature of our humanity, constantly struggling between the twin polarities of darkness and light, goodness and selfishness.

And that, dear reader is the story of the story. I hope you enjoy this dark little fairy tale. If you do, let me know. There may be more.

Keep an eye on the water. Something is sure to come out of it.

# *One*

Petra awoke with the early sunlight streaming through the tatters of her curtains, painting golden patterns over the bed and the dingy, mostly bare walls. For the moment, the golden sun-patterns transformed the room into something quiet and cheerful. It made Petra just a little sad as she laid in her bed, blinking slowly, her dark hair spread haphazardly over her pillow, because she knew it wasn't a true picture. Still, it was nice in the moment. In the moment, before the unpleasant bustle of the morning began, she tried to enjoy it.

There were quiet footsteps outside her not-quite-closed bedroom door. A shadow moved in the dimness of the hall. Petra smiled very slightly.

"Petra," a girl's voice whispered. "I left Beatrice in your room. Can I come get her?"

Petra sighed and rolled over, raising herself onto her elbow. "Yes, come in. Be quiet, though."

"I know," the girl replied, still whispering. She pushed the door open slowly, trying to prevent it from creaking but creaking it all the more. Petra's sad smile grew a bit wider as she watched. The younger girl had golden hair and pale features, despite her suntanned cheeks and nose. Slowly, she crept into the room, scanning the floor, her eyes serious. Doll's clothes were scattered on the bare floorboards at the foot of the bed. The girl spied something and her eyes widened. She ducked, disappearing behind the footboard and reappearing a moment later with a small, bedraggled doll clutched to her chest.

"I was worried about her," the girl whispered, glancing down at the doll in her arms. "She doesn't like being by herself at night. She wants to sleep with me. I forgot her after we were done playing last night, but I tried to send her happy thoughts, because I couldn't come back for her after nights out. I told her in my thoughts that she'd be all right and not to be afraid and that I'd come for her in the morning. It worked, too, see? She's still happy." The girl turned the doll around, showing Petra the big stitched smile on the doll's face.

Petra nodded, amused. "She's happy because her mama loves her so much. What's she have to worry about? Better get her back to your room before your mother hears you, though. If she knows we're up already…"

"I can be real quiet," the girl stated gravely. "Watch."

With exaggerated care, the girl began to creep back out of the room, raising her feet as if she were stepping over landmines. Petra couldn't help grinning at her. At the door, the girl stopped and turned back. "Tonight again, Petra? Before nights out? You be Astra this time and Mr. Bobkins can be Treus. I'll be the Marsh Hag, 'kay?"

Petra shook her head, more in amusement than negation. "Don't you ever get tired of that story, Iz?"

The girl shook her own head vigorously. "Before nights out," she said again, making Petra promise. A moment later she was gone, and she was, indeed, remarkably quiet as she crept back to her bedroom. From below, Petra could hear clankings and mutterings from the kitchen. It wouldn't be long before Phyllis would call up for Petra and Izzy, hollering the beginning of the day. If that happened, things would start badly.

*"I was worried about her," the girl whispered,*
*glancing down at the doll in her arms.*

Phyllis liked her schedule adhered to, and if she had to call the two girls downstairs, it was a sign that they had already fallen behind for the day. Phyllis hated lollygagging, as she called it. She hated scampering, which is what she called it whenever Izzy played or explored. Phyllis wasn't Petra's mother, or even her grandmother, who had died years ago. Phyllis wasn't even a witch. She was, however, Petra's grandfather's wife, and she was, despite all appearances, Izzy's mother.

Sighing, Petra swung her legs out of bed and crossed the floor to her wardrobe, enjoying the last few minutes of quiet and the bright coins of sunlight that sprayed cheerfully through the tattered curtains, as if falling on a happy home and a happy girl. Petra was not a very happy girl. Even as she picked out her clothes, the night's dream circled her head, dark and buzzing, like a cloud of flies. She had the dream almost every night now, to the point that she'd almost gotten used to it. It wasn't even a dream, really, but a memory playing over and over, like a taunt. In it, Petra saw her own mother, her birth mother, whom she had never known. The dream mother smiled, and it was the same sad smile Petra so often smiled herself when she looked at her step-sister Izzy. In the dream, Petra heard her own voice cry out, "I'm sorry, Mum!" and every time, the dreaming-Petra tried to drown out the memory-Petra, to cut off that declaration, to overrule it. Always, she couldn't, and as the memory-Petra's voice rang out, the figure of her mother would disintegrate. She would collapse like a water sculpture, splashing in on herself and running over the floor, coursing into a greenly flickering pool from which Petra knew she would never reappear. The dreaming-Petra tried to shout in anguish and despair, but she could make no sound. In the dream, out of the darkness, another voice spoke instead. It was wheedling and maddening. Petra tried not to listen to it. It was a dead voice. But it was getting harder not to hear. Sometimes, in fact, Petra even heard it when she was awake. She heard it in the back rooms of her own mind, as if it was a part of her. Petra was afraid of the things the dark voice said. Not because she didn't agree with them, but because part of her—a secret, buried, deep-down part of her—did.

Petra sighed, gathered her clothes and crept down the hall to the bathroom.

"We've a very busy day before us, girls," Phyllis said brusquely as Petra and Izzy entered the kitchen. "Five more minutes' lollygagging up there and you'd not have had time for breakfast. You are aware that I do not approve of slothfulness."

"Sorry Mother," Izzy said dutifully, climbing onto a chair at the table. Petra sat next to her and eyed her plate; one piece of dry toast, cut in half, and a dollop of plain yogurt. Phyllis was a staunch believer in healthy foods. Her own sticklike frame was a testament to it, and she was fiercely proud of her fitness. Silently, Petra pined for the breakfasts in the Great Hall, the sausages and pancakes and fresh kippers. She reminded herself that those days were officially over. Graduation had been a week past. Neither Phyllis nor Izzy had attended, of course, but Petra's grandfather had been there, wearing his one good brown suit, which had probably been fashionable sometime in the middle of the previous century. It was hard to say if he'd been proud of Petra as she accepted her diploma from headmaster Merlinus, but he'd at least been there, his bushy eyebrows knitted into something resembling a dutiful scowl of approval.

Phyllis interrupted Petra's thoughts with her strident, buzz-saw voice. "Your grandfather has asked for you to accompany him to the south field this morning, Petra, do not make him wait. Izabella, you know what today is, I assume."

Izzy glanced up at Petra, her eyes wide. Petra mouthed the word 'goats'.

"Goats," Izzy answered, slumping. "Not the goats. Please."

"We've been through this, Izabella," Phyllis sang condescendingly. "If we don't trim their horns, the beasts will harm themselves. It's for their own good, as you well know. I'll not have another word about it."

Izzy was afraid of her mother, but she roused herself. "But they *bleed* when I do it. I don't want to hurt them! Let Petra do it. She can always do it without hurting them."

Phyllis bristled and glared at Petra for a moment. "That's because Petra is an insolent practitioner of unnaturalness. We'll have none of that infernal witchery in this house, as you well know. Whatever your sister chose to do at that awful school is her business entirely, but those days are over, and none too soon. It's high time your sister found something *useful* to do with her life. I'll allow none of that sort of thing under *my* roof, and her grandfather is in complete agreement with me."

"But Mother," Izzy said, pushing her plate away. "I'm *scared* of the goats,"

"That is because you are simple, Izabella," her mother said matter-of-factly. "And it is my duty to force you to overcome that defect. It's bad enough that you were born this way. I'll not coddle you even further into your natural stupidity. I've had a hard enough time finding a place in life for you. How would you like it if the Percival Sunnyton Work Farm refused you because you were too soft-headed to be able to handle a saw?"

Izzy didn't respond. She stared down at her chest, her lip pooched out. Finally, she shook her head.

"It's entirely possible," Phyllis said breezily, whisking Izzy's barely touched breakfast away and clattering the plate into the sink. "Just *think* what a disappointment you'd be to me and your step-father. After all we've done for you. Mr. Sunnyton won't pay you much, but it's the best we can hope for, and it certainly isn't as if we can't use the income. And as you well know, it really is your only chance in life. After all, what else is a dim little thing like you good for?"

Petra seethed but didn't say anything. She knew from experience that defending Izzy only made matters worse. Instead, she caught Izzy's eye when Phyllis turned her back. She allowed a smile to curl the corner of her lips and raised her wrist slightly. Izzy looked up at Petra, her lip still pooched out, and then saw the small wooden shaft protruding ever-so-slightly from the sleeve of Petra's work dress. Izzy immediately grinned and covered her mouth with her hands. She shook her head from side to side, warning Petra, but her eyes sparkled encouragingly. Surreptitiously, Petra raised her arm, pretending to stretch. Across the kitchen, Phyllis reached for the faucet of the sink, meaning to start the morning dishes. Suddenly, the base of the faucet spurted a jet of water, as if it had sprung a leak. Phyllis spluttered and scrambled backwards as the water struck her squarely in the face. Izzy smothered laughter into her hands as Petra lowered her arm, slipping her wand back up her sleeve. From the doorway behind them came the noise of someone clearing his throat. Both Petra and Izzy jumped guiltily and turned.

"Work's awaiting," Petra's grandfather said from the hall entrance, eyeing her closely, unsmiling. He was dressed in his old, scuffed trousers and a heavy shirt. His mostly bald head was red from the sun.

"Warren," Phyllis spat angrily. "This sink is acting up again. How am I supposed to function with such defective tools? As if Izabella wasn't bad enough. I thought you fixed this leak!"

"Seems some leaks are worse than others," Petra's grandfather said, his eyes still on Petra. "One thing at a time, woman. I'll address it upon my return. Come, Petra."

As Petra stood up from the table, she palmed a piece of leftover toast from her plate. She skirted the table, passing the toast to Izzy. The younger girl took it and grinned, biting off a corner.

"I'm glad you thought to bring your stick with you," Petra's grandfather said pointedly as the wagon bounced over the rutted path, pulled by the farm's single, geriatric horse. In the back of the wagon, farm tools and bags of fertilizer bounced and creaked.

"It's not a stick, grandfather," Petra said tiredly. "It's a wand. Call it what it is."

"You shouldn't pique the woman of the house," Grandfather muttered. "It doesn't make things any easier for anyone."

Petra sighed. They'd had this conversation many times before. "What about you? You're the one who asks me to come with you so I can magic the rocks out of the field and knit the fences back together. What if she finds out about that?"

"She won't," grandfather answered calmly. "I won't tell because I appreciate your help too much, and you won't tell because it gives you the only outlet for your abilities."

"My abilities?" Petra said, glancing at him. "What about you? Have you completely forgotten who you are?"

"Just because you're my granddaughter is no excuse for insolence," the older man said impassively, snapping the reins. Petra knew enough of her grandfather's past to know that he was stubbornly opposed to even discussing it. Unlike other couples of mixed magical stock, Phyllis had discovered Warren Morganstern's true magical identity early on, and had disapproved vigorously, so much so that as an agreement for marriage, Phyllis had insisted that her wizard fiancé denounce his magic and break his own wand.

"I've made my choices," Petra's grandfather went on after a few moments' silence. "You may not understand them, but you don't need to. Soon enough you'll be gone and need not think of Phyllis or me ever again. In fact, considering everything, I'm surprised you came back here at all, now that your schooling's done and you're of age."

Petra didn't respond to that. The truth was, she didn't know why she had come back. She'd always assumed that, once she came of age, she'd never again set foot in the house she'd grown up in, and good riddance. And yet, once her graduation had come and gone, almost without realizing it, Petra had found herself back in the narrow bed in the cold, barren room she'd known her entire life. She wanted to leave, wanted to break away and find a new life, and yet, for reasons she didn't at all understand, each day found her still here. Perhaps it was Izzy. Petra had always looked out for her as well as she could. The girl was indeed simple, as Phyllis reminded her every day, but she wasn't stupid. Her childlikeness was secretly delightful to Petra, who took every rare opportunity to play with the girl, fleetingly and unbeknownst to Phyllis, before what Izzy called "nights out" each evening. Izzy was the only person who Petra could talk to about magic, although they had to keep it a sworn secret. Izzy loved Petra's stories about the magical school, with classes of levitation, and broom flying, and changing things into other things. She'd delighted in Petra's accounts of the wizarding play, the Triumvirate, in which Petra had played a part during her final year of school. During their fleeting moments of free time, Petra and Izzy would walk around the small lake at the edge of the property. There, hidden from the house by a stand of woods, Petra would do small magic for Izzy, levitating her dolls and making them dance, or transfiguring pebbles into tiny butterflies as Izzy threw them into the air. Once, Petra and Izzy had sat on the edge of the tiny dock, swinging their legs and watching the dragonflies stitch patterns over the rippling waves, and there they had talked about Petra's mysterious magical heritage.

"Where did you come from, Petra?" Izzy asked, looking up at her and squinting in the afternoon sun.

"I don't know, really," Petra had answered. "Your step-father... doesn't like to talk about it."

"Is Papa Warren a wizard?"

Petra shrugged lightly and looked out over the water.

"I wish I was a witch, like you," Izzy said, leaning back on her pudgy little hands. "But I'm not, am I?"

Petra turned and smiled at her step-sister. "I wouldn't be too sure, Iz. The way you can send thoughts to your dollies. That's kind of witchy, don't you think?"

Izzy screwed up her face thoughtfully. Finally, she said, "It's a *little* witchy, but not really. But I'm not really a Muddle either."

Petra had long since stopped correcting Izzy about magical terminology. She shook her head. "No, you're not really a Muddle, either, Iz. Too much magic in you for that."

"I'm right in the middle," Izzy said firmly, sitting up again. "Stuck between being a witch and a Muddle. That's not so bad, is it?"

"I guess that makes you a Wuddle, then, doesn't it?" Petra said, smiling crookedly.

"I'm a Wuddle," Izzy agreed. "A widdle Wuddle."

Petra shook her head, laughing, and pushed Izzy, as if to throw her into the lake. Together, the two girls wrestled and giggled playfully as the sun lowered over the lake, burnishing its surface, turning it slowly into gold.

"Phyllis is complaining about the spiders," Petra's grandfather said, braking the wagon with a jerk and snapping Petra out of her reverie.

"The what?" she asked, blinking.

"Spiders," her grandfather repeated, climbing down to the dirt path. "Down on the dock. You know she likes to take her tea there some afternoons. I was thinking perhaps you'd clean it up for her."

Petra narrowed her eyes at her grandfather. "How did you know I was thinking about the dock?"

Warren Morganstern glanced at his granddaughter. "I didn't know any such thing. Phyllis mentioned it earlier this morning, that's all. Don't you go getting rumours started that I'm some sort of mentalist or I'll never hear the end of it."

It was his idea of a joke, but Petra didn't smile. The fact was that she knew her grandfather couldn't completely deny his wizarding blood, even if he had broken his own wand in two pieces and burnt them in the woodstove (and what a colorful fire *that* had been). The wand didn't make the wizard any more than an envelope makes a letter. Warren Morganstern could indeed read minds, at least in a vague, murky sense, and this ability seemed only to have increased as he'd denied every other expression of his magical nature. Petra didn't think he even knew it himself, but she'd seen his ability in action on countless occasions. It was in the way that he'd come back from the fields with a hand-picked bouquet of wildflowers for Phyllis on the very days when she'd been the most snappish and mean, the flowers cooling her just enough to make the evening bearable. It was in the little comments he'd make to the clerk at the market, who had a tendency to stick his thumb on the scales of everyone else's orders, but never grandfathers. It was in the timing of the few words of praise or stilted affection he offered to Izzy or even Petra herself; rare, but always when they were most needed and appreciated. Grandfather was not a strong-hearted man, but he wasn't mean. And he was still, in spite of Phyllis and his own willing renunciation, a wizard.

"Don't you have some kind of death spray to kill the spiders?" Petra groused, climbing down from the wagon and producing her wand from her sleeve. "The hardware store has aisles full of that kind of thing, don't they?"

"Your way's neater," her grandfather replied, walking out into the field. "Not to mention cheaper."

Petra sighed and followed her grandfather. They were still within sight of the house, near the top of a hill overlooking the entire farm. At least the morning would allow her some small pleasure, levitating the rocks that had been pulled out of the ground by Grandfather's till. There was already a substantial pile of them at the base of a large, gnarled tree in the center of the field—the "Wishing Tree", as Izzy called it for no obvious reason. Phyllis had assumed that Warren and Petra were lugging the rocks by hand, and was self-centered enough not to give it a second though. That was good, since, if she'd paid closer attention, she'd have seen that some of the rocks in the pile would've been more accurately described as boulders. Many of them were far heavier than even a fit man could lift, much less a scrawny seventy-year old and a teenage girl.

Warren pointed, and Petra saw a smooth dome of brown rock protruding slightly from the tilled earth. It had a bright scratch on it where the tiller had scarred it, and Petra thought for a moment that it looked like the skull of a buried murder victim. The thought did not dismay her, as she knew it should. She pointed her wand and flicked. The rock tore out of the earth with a sort of wet, ripping sound and

*The rock tore out of the earth with a sort of wet,
ripping sound and hovered in the air, turning slowly,
bits of moist earth pattering off of it.*

hovered in the air, turning slowly, bits of moist earth pattering off of it. Petra stared at it. It wasn't a skull, and Petra realized, idly, that she was a little disappointed.

There was no official gravesite for Petra's parents, not as far as she was concerned. She now knew that they *were*, in fact, buried somewhere, but that didn't constitute a gravesite. Not really. For one thing, they weren't buried together, as a husband and wife should be. Her mother, who'd died giving birth to Petra, was buried in some seedy forgotten cemetery in London. Petra didn't even know the name of it, and had never been there. She didn't want to go, either. She didn't want to see her mother's name engraved on just one more headstone, crowded in with dozens of others, leaning and cracked, like rotting teeth. Her father, on the other hand, was interred in an anonymous catacomb beneath the wizard prison that had been his final, tragic home. She'd only recently learned of this, in her last year of school, on her birthday. Her father had been killed while imprisoned, vengeance mistakenly taken upon him by the guards for "protecting" villains her father could not even name. No one had claimed his body, and it had simply been dumped in the honeycomb of caves beneath the prison, along with the other forgotten inmates who'd died within those horrible walls. Petra couldn't bear to think of it; her parents, misused and manipulated, crushed to death in the gears of a battle they didn't even understand, and instantly forgotten by both sides of that battle, immediately trampled underfoot as the war waged on, senselessly and stupidly. Deep down, Petra hated both sides.

Thus, she had made her own gravesite for her parents. Years and years ago, when she had been very small, Petra had found a small hollow in the wood that separated the farmhouse from the tiny lake, and there, her small, child's mind had decided she would make their gravesite. She did not then understand what a gravesite meant. She only knew that her parents were dead, and dead people were given stone monuments, like totems, to help others to remember them. She knew that her parents' monuments should be together, so that they could comfort each other in death. Without thinking about it, Petra moved stones into position for the graves, stacking them carefully, without ever touching them. Young Petra was acquainted with magic even then, and she called upon it to form her parents' grave monuments, never telling anyone what she was doing. Petra's magic tended to upset people, although she didn't understand why. After all, Grandmother and Grandfather were magical. She had seen them use magic loads of times around the farm and the house, had watched how grandfather could make the interior of the old lake gazebo at the end of the dock much larger on the inside than the outside, so that they could have parties inside if they wished. And yet Petra's magic seemed to frighten her grandparents for some reason. As a result, Petra had learned not to use it in front of them. She used her hands to carry the buckets of milk from the stable to the house, rather than making them float along, which was much more fun. She closed the parlor curtains by pulling the cord, rather than simply thinking them shut. And she definitely didn't use her thoughts to kill the rats in the cellar, even though they scared her so much, with their flashing eyes in the darkness, skittering amongst the burlap sacks of potatoes and beets. Petra would never forget the white face of her grandmother when she had come up from the cellar that morning, the day after Petra had first realized that she could think the rats to death. Her grandmother had merely taken Petra by the hand, led her outside to the poplar tree, pulled off a long switch, and swatted Petra smartly on the hand; five stinging strikes, one for each dead rat on the cellar's dirt floor. Petra knew that her grandmother was afraid of the rats nearly as much as she herself was, and yet her grandmother's white face and the thin red line of her mouth told Petra that, in that moment, inexplicably, her grandmother was even more afraid of the crying little girl in front of her.

Thus, secretly, young Petra had moved the stones from the ground for her parents' graves, wandless, merely pointing the fingers of her small hands. Levitating them effortlessly, she stacked the stones, fitting them perfectly together, until there were two piles, two stone cairns, each slightly taller than the little girl who had made them. Young Petra felt a little better, then. The gravesite seemed right and just. Whenever Petra felt particularly alone or fearful, she would sneak out to the makeshift gravesite. Even before grandmother had died, before the magic had gone from the farm and the horrible Phyllis had come to live with them, even before the gazebo had broken off the end of the dock and crashed into the lake, unable to support itself without grandfather's magic, Petra would steal out to the hollow in the woods. Countless times, all throughout her growing up years, Petra would come, often sneaking out in the middle of the night. She would sit on a large fallen tree before the stone cairns, and talk to them, her long lost parents, whom she had never known, whose faces she wouldn't even recognize.

Petra was much taller than the stone cairns now, but she still came sometimes, as she had now. She still sat on the ancient fallen tree, which had long since settled into a drift of wildflowers and blowing grass. She even still talked to her parents sometimes, but rarely aloud anymore.

Unlike the little Petra who had built the graves, grown-up Petra knew that her parents couldn't hear her anymore. And also unlike the little Petra who had built the graves, grown-up Petra now knew what her long-dead parents looked like. She had seen their faces dozens of times during the previous year, enough times to burn them into her memory. She had seen them looking out at her from the waters of a secret magical pool, their faces sad but loving, and in the pool they had been together. That was an important part of the memory. They had been together in the mysterious pool, and Petra had a secret sense that that was because of the gravesite she had built; the stone cairns had joined her parents in death, and she was glad of it. In the pool's greenish reflection, Petra had seen that her parents had been handsome people, albeit simple; good at heart, but gullible. Petra did not hate them for this. One does not hate a rabbit because it is too simple to avoid walking into a trap. One pities the rabbit, and hates the murderers who set the trap, who are willing to take advantage of the rabbit's humble naiveté, and for no reason other than to use and kill.

Petra sat in front of the graves, thinking of her parents' faces, imagining that she could see them in the very rocks of their grave cairns. The packed stones had never come apart or loosened. In fact, a netting of flowering vines had grown over the cairns, strengthening them and making them beautiful. Petra could no longer remember if she had made the vines grow there using her magic, but she thought it was likely. She never had to place flowers on her parents' graves, because the vines always bloomed when she wanted them to; dark red flowers with yellow stamens, lush and vibrant, beautifully fragrant. Even in the dead of winter, when the rest of the wood was a black and white tableau of barrenness, the vines could be made to flower whenever Petra wished. She didn't always make it happen, but sometimes it felt right. Sometimes it felt necessary.

As the afternoon sun filtered through the trees, painting moving patterns on the graves, Petra did not make the flowers bloom. She didn't know if she ever would again. She had seen the faces of her dead parents in the water, and had made the choice not to draw them out of that water, not to bring them back into the world of the living. Perhaps the very promise of their return had been a lie. Petra tried to convince herself that it had merely been an evil trick, that *no* magic could ever truly bring her parents back, despite her greatest wish. But she had seen her mother climbing out of that pool, had seen her standing there, solid and real, her face smiling with love, watching Petra. She still saw it nearly every night in her dream, and watched that ultimate moment when she, the dream-Petra, chose to deny that return. It had seemed like the brave and right thing to do at the time—to deny herself her deepest desire in order to save another's life.

Even now, as Petra stared unseeingly at the secret gravesite of her parents, Petra knew it had been the right choice. But why, then, did she feel so very, very lost? Why did she struggle with such a crushing, haunting sense of loss? Why, most of all, did she feel the horrible weight of fear that somehow, in some monumental way, she had failed her long-lost parents?

The wind blew, skirling dead leaves through the tall grass and singing a high note in the canopy of trees, in the very vines that embraced the twin graves. Petra stared at the graves, her blue eyes large and sparkling, unseeing, lost in the dream and the maddening words of the voice in the back rooms of her mind.

She did not make the red flowers bloom.

*Petra sat in front of the graves, thinking of
her parents' faces, imagining that she could see them
in the very rocks of their grave cairns.*

That evening, after scrubbing the dinner dishes and cleaning the kitchen with Izzy's help, Petra announced that she was going for a walk out to the lake.

"Suit yourself," Phyllis replied indistinctly, the corner of her lips pinched around a pair of pins as she hemmed one of Izzy's dresses. "Don't forget to sweep the stoop before you go mooning about in your room for the rest of the night. I'll not see that mess of dirt you and your grandfather tracked up to the door when I go out in the morning."

Petra pressed her lips together but didn't respond. The screen door clapped as she left, walking out into the reddening evening light. A moment later, there was the screech and clap of the screen door again as Izzy ran out, following Petra. Petra smiled a little, slowing her pace without looking back. Izzy caught up to her and matched her pace, stepping gingerly over patches of heather.

"Your mother knows you're coming with me?" Petra asked after a moment.

Izzy nodded. "She doesn't need me until she's done hemming my new work dress. She wants me to try it on before nights out, 'cuz it's her only chance to get the fit right before I leave for Mr. Sunnyton's next week. But night's out isn't for another hour, so she said I could come if we hurried back. And she said to tell you not to let me near the dock 'cuz I'll fall in 'cuz I'm clumsy as a two-legged stool and I swim like a cobblestone."

Petra felt the heat rise in her cheeks again, but only looked down at Izzy and ruffled her hair. For reasons Petra could not begin to understand, Izzy loved her mother, seamlessly and without question. She trusted everything Phyllis said, even when it was insulting and degrading to Izzy. Of course, it was true that Izzy was not particularly smart. She'd been born with a defect that Petra didn't understand, except that it made Izzy slower to grasp things than other children her age. On the other hand, however, the same 'defect' seemed to have given Izzy a beautifully sweet and simple disposition. The girl was unflaggingly loyal, trusting and affectionate, even to Phyllis, when she was allowed to be. Somehow, she completely failed to see that her own mother barely approved of her, and was even ashamed of her. Rarely did Phyllis allow Izzy to accompany her into town, and when she did, Izzy was forbidden to speak, and was commanded to walk immediately behind Phyllis, staying "out of the way and out of trouble".

"Are you happy to start working at Mr. Sunnyton's Work Farm next week?" Petra asked lightly.

Izzy drew a huge sigh. "Yes, I guess so. What if it's really hard, though?"

Petra shrugged and didn't say anything.

"Mother says I'll only have to stay there during the week. That means I can come home on Saturday and Sunday, and see everybody and have time to scamper around a bit. Mother says Mr. Sunnyton doesn't allow any scampering around at the work farm, even before nights out. Do you think that's true?"

Petra walked on, staring at the tall grass that bordered the path. "I imagine you'll have some time to scamper, Iz. You may have to make the time for yourself, but you can be smart about it. Maybe after dinner, like we do here sometimes."

Izzy considered this. After a moment, she brightened a bit. "If I was a witch, I'd be starting school instead of going to Mr. Sunnyton's, wouldn't I"

Petra nodded, unsmiling.

"That would be wonderful," Izzy enthused. "I could get my own magic wand and learn to do amazing stuff. Mother thinks she doesn't like magic, but if I was a witch, she'd see different, I think. She'd see how nice it was to have a magical daughter who could help her around the farm. I'd learn of all sorts of new ways to make things happen by magic, so she'd not have to work so hard. That would make her happy, don't you think?"

Petra drew a deep sigh. "You're probably right, Iz."

"Mother says school's not all it is cracked up to be, though," Izzy said, jumping over a tree root. "Especially for someone like me. She says I should be happy I don't have to go, because I'd just see how different I was from the other little girls and boys."

Petra pressed her lips together tightly. Finally, just as the two of them rounded the reach of the woods, she said, "So should I not let you out on the dock with me?"

"No, I think it's all right," Izzy replied, tilting her head in a caricature of thoughtfulness. "I'll stay in the middle, like always. You'll keep a watch on me. Mother won't know."

As they approached the dock, the lake laid silent and glassy smooth, reflecting the red sky like an enormous mirror. Petra stopped at the steps leading down to the dock.

"I'm going to be killing the spiders, Iz," she said, glancing back at the girl. "Will that bother you?"

"Ugh, no," Izzy answered with feeling. "I hate them. They just sit there in the middle of their webs staring at me as I go past, bobbing back and forth when the wind blows, like they wish I was small enough to get stuck in their web so they could get to me. I hate the spiders."

"Spiders aren't bad, Iz," Petra said idly, stepping onto the warped wood of the old dock. "They're not interested in you. They catch lots of other bugs that are a lot worse. Mosquitoes *do* want to bite you, but there are a lot less of them, because the spiders eat them."

Izzy shivered and hugged herself, standing on the first step of the dock. "I don't mind them when I can't see them, like the ones out in the field. I just don't like the ones out here. They look at me."

Petra produced her wand and smiled crookedly at her step-sister. "They won't be looking at you much longer. This'll only take a few minutes. Why don't you stay back there and not watch, all right, Iz?"

Izzy nodded fervently and turned around. Almost instantly, she became distracted by a strew of white rocks near the shore. She began to pry them up and toss them into the lake, making interlaced patterns of ripple rings on its smooth surface.

Petra sighed and pointed her wand. She was no longer able to merely think the spiders to death, as she had when she was young. Back then, just like with the rats, she'd been able to see right into the minds of the tiny creatures, find that one spark of life, like a candle in a cave, and simply pinch it out. She'd always been good at understanding how bodies worked and how they were put together. Because of that, throughout her life on the farm, almost nobody had gotten particularly sick or been seriously injured. Grandfather worked far harder than a man his age should be able to, and yet each morning he awoke fresh and limber, without any lingering soreness. There was no arthritis in his or Phyllis' joints, no brittle bones or weak hearts or lungs. When Petra was young, she did her secret work on the adults' bodies without even really trying. She assumed it was simply the role of the child to maintain the adults, to peek into them from across the room, find the weaknesses, and carefully encourage their bodies to repair them. If only young Petra had understood the nature of cancer, she might have been able to save her grandmother's life. She'd seen the darkness there, growing inside her grandmother's body, but she couldn't get inside it, couldn't work out what it was or whether it was good or bad. Grandmother eventually went to the doctors, but neither she nor grandfather told young Petra about the cancer that was eating her away. Soon enough, grandmother died, and her entire body had gone dark to Petra. The young girl felt some responsibility for it, but not much. She was a remarkably pragmatic girl, and even in her sorrow, there was some small anger at her grandparents. Why hadn't they told Petra about grandmother's illness so she could try to fix it? It seemed so foolish and destructive to have kept it a secret. And then, gradually, Petra began to understand that her grandparents *didn't know* about her special talents. They had no idea that she could see inside them and help their bodies. And then, on the heels of that realization, it occurred to young Petra that maybe it was best if they *didn't* know. Maybe it would only frighten them, like so much of Petra's other magic. For the first time, Petra began to understand why her magic might worry others. After all, if she could use her mind to get inside their bodies to help them, maybe they were afraid that she might decide to use the same skills to hurt them. Like she had with the rats. But, of course, Petra knew in her heart that she would never do that to the people who cared for her. Why should they worry about that? What had Petra ever done to make them fear her that way?

Either way, young Petra decided it would be best not to tell them about this special kind of magic; the inside-the-body magic. Like the levitating and the moving things with her mind, she began doing less and less of it. And slowly, over time, she began to forget how to do those things at all. She began to lose her grasp of the secret mental muscles that made the magic happen. Now, she merely soothed her grandfather's joints and muscles, and took care that Phyllis had no major pains in her fingers and knees, where she was prone to rheumatism. Petra didn't do this because she cared for Phyllis, but because, for reasons Petra could never guess, her grandfather did.

Petra could no longer simply think the dock spiders to death, like she had when she was young. Now, she had to use her wand, but even so, she didn't have to say the curses out loud. Few people knew this. Petra had learned to keep many of her skills a secret, even from her friends and teachers at school. She was quite good at casting spells with only her thoughts, even if she did need her wand to make them happen. Slowly, Petra paced along the dock, pointing her wand at the webs which festooned the pilings and producing tiny, almost imperceptible green flashes. The spiders dropped dead from their webs, their legs clenched into tight curlicues. As grandfather had implied, there was quite a number of them. By the time Petra reached the furthest end of the dock, where the old lake gazebo had once been attached, the weathered planks were littered with lifeless spiders.

"Are they all dead?" Izzy called, still refusing to look at the dock from her position on the rocky shoreline. "I don't want to see them."

"They're dead," Petra answered. "You can come up in a minute."

She retraced her steps along the dock, stepping over the dead spiders and fingering her wand. At the base of the dock, she turned around and pointed her wand again. Without a word, a jet of air began to blow from its tip. Petra used it to blow the tiny carcasses toward the end of the dock, thinking rather morbidly that the curled legs made them look like tiny black and brown tumbleweeds. Petra's skin crawled a little at the sight of it, but only a little. By the time she reached the end of the dock, the sun had dipped completely below the horizon, painting the sky a bright, burnt red and turning the lake into a mirror of blood. Petra flicked her wand, sending the cloud of dead spiders skittering off the end of the dock and into the water. She watched them strike the surface, where they floated and then, slowly, began to sink.

As the spiders drifted down into the dark depths, something else seemed to rise up to the surface, shimmering, almost glowing, ever-so-faint.

Petra's face didn't change, but her heart stopped for a long moment, and then began to pound, struggling to catch up to her racing thoughts. It had to be a trick of the light, or simply her own overactive imagination. She'd been dreaming the dream for so long now that it was leaking over into her waking daydreams. That *had* to be it. There was simply no way that she could really be seeing the shape that seemed to be arising, drifting just under the sunset-tinted surface of the water. It was a face. Petra recognized it, of course. She could almost convince herself it was merely a trick of the light, simply a strange complexity of twilight and shadows beneath the water's surface, produced by the faint outlines of the derelict gazebo that lay dead on the lake's bottom directly below her.

But it wasn't. It was Petra's mother. Her face looked up at Petra, just as it had from the greenly flickering pool during her last school year. Petra had believed she would never see that face again, apart from her dreams, but there it was, ghostly faint, almost lost in the shadows of the depths.

*It was the spiders*, Petra thought suddenly, her heart hammering, her face still blank as she stared down, eyes wide. *The spiders! I killed them and sent them into the water, just like I was supposed to have done in the chamber of the pool.* Only then, the death was supposed to have been a murder, a human sacrifice. "Blood for blood", the voice in the back rooms of her mind had said. "That is the only way to fulfill the requirements and bring balance. That is the only way to bring your parents back." The spiders weren't enough to fulfill that bargain, but they *were* enough to produce the faintest, shimmering reflection.

"What do you see?" Izzy said suddenly, her voice coming from directly behind Petra. Petra gasped and turned around, realizing she hadn't taken a breath for the past several seconds.

*She could almost convince herself it was merely a trick of the light...*

Izzy stopped suddenly in the middle of the dock, her eyes widening. "What? What is it, Petra?"

Petra forced her voice to sound normal. "Nothing. I was just looking. You can still see the gazebo down there when the lighting is just right. It's... a little creepy."

"Neat," Izzy said, stepping forward again to join Petra on the end of the dock. "I like creepy. Let me see it."

When the girls looked down, the lighting had changed slightly. Petra was relieved to see that the shimmery image of her mother's face was gone.

*If it was ever really there*, part of Petra's mind said. *You imagined it. It wasn't real. It was* never *real.* But the voice had no power. Petra knew what she had seen. She was surprised that the phantom voice from the back rooms of her mind was silent now, but she sensed that it was there nonetheless, alert, watching, waiting.

"I see it," Izzy whispered, pointing tentatively. "Down there. It's still there, even though we thought it was gone. See?"

Petra nodded slowly. Matching Izzy's conspiratorial whisper, she said, "I do, Izzy. I can still see it."

# Two

The next day was Saturday, and while Phyllis didn't usually observe any difference between the weekend and any other day of the week, she was even more brusque than usual as Izzy and Petra made their way down the stairs.

"Eat as you walk, Izabella," Phyllis stated flatly, shoving a plate of cold toast toward the girl without looking at her. "No, no, don't take the entire plate, you dim thing, just one piece, and no time for jam. You'll make a mess of it at any rate. Run along down to the barn and sweep all the stalls, first thing. I want it done by the time Warren is done with Bethel."

Petra tightened her lips. Bethel was the family's milk cow, and Grandfather was surely already there. Sweeping the stalls before he finished milking her was an impossibility.

"I'll do it," Petra spoke up, snatching a piece of toast from the plate and heading for the door.

"Oh, no you don't, young lady," Phyllis said sharply. "I know how *you* sweep. I'd sooner have you locked in the closet than out there for anyone to see. I have a *special* task for you today."

"But Mother," Izzy said, "I just finished sweeping the barn yesterday."

"I just cooked dinner yesterday, too, didn't I?" Phyllis replied, stacking pans in a tall cabinet and slamming the door. "But sure enough you'll be mooching around here tonight looking for another one, won't you? Life is work, Izabella. If you don't know that by now, then you're slower than I thought. Now go!" Phyllis' eyes flashed as she barked the last word, and Izzy turned on her heel like a scared puppy, forgetting even to grab a piece of the dry toast. As the side door squeaked and clapped shut, Petra glared at Phyllis from across the table, her eyes narrowed and her hands clenched into loose fists.

"Oh, don't you start," Phyllis said, dismissing her and turning to the sink. "It isn't as if you have any stake in the matter. I can't even begin to imagine why you are even still here, but as long as you can't find anything useful to do with your life, I'll be happy to keep you occupied. The least you can do is earn your own keep. Today you'll walk to the market and ask Mr. Thurman for store credit for a new trunk. Nothing special, mind you, just something big enough for Izabella's work dresses and some necessities. I won't have her dragging those silly dolls of hers along with her to the work farm."

Petra shook her head slightly, so full of things to say that she couldn't say anything. Phyllis ignored her.

There was no chance that Mr. Thurman was going to extend any more credit to the Morgansterns, no matter who asked for it, and Phyllis knew it. Getting the trunk wasn't really the point, anyway. Phyllis' plan was simply to get rid of Petra for the day. Mr. Sunnyton, owner of the nearby work farm, was coming today to meet and evaluate Izzy. It was the closest thing to a job interview that workers at the farm ever got, and Petra knew it'd be more like a livestock auction than an interview. The thought of it boiled her very blood. Phyllis knew this, of course, and knew that Petra would find it impossible not to interfere when the time came. Thus, she'd arranged to send Petra off on a useless errand, one that would take her most of the day.

"Don't think about talking to your grandfather about this, my dear," Phyllis commented, as if reading Petra's thoughts. "He is in complete agreement with me. Off with you, now, before I decide to make you carry back a sack of flour with you."

Petra still didn't move. She stared at the back of Phyllis' head, her anger smouldering, banking into a bright little furnace of hate. Petra almost relished it. It focused her. It wouldn't always be like this, she thought for the millionth time. Someday, things would change. Someday, the scales would balance and good would win out. It was the nature of the drama of life, wasn't it? Good always won in the end. It was the only thing Petra had to hang onto. After all, Petra's choice to side with good in the chamber of the pool had cost her her greatest desire. The force of Good owed her, didn't it? It owed her plenty.

Petra took a deep, measured breath and turned to leave the kitchen. As she reached the stairs, Phyllis interrupted her once more.

"And Petra," she said, leaning to meet Petra's eyes through the kitchen doorway, her gaze implacable. "You'll *walk* to the market. Do you understand me?"

Petra held Phyllis' gaze for several seconds, keeping her own face entirely blank. She neither nodded nor shook her head, but Phyllis had made her point very clear: *no magic*. Finally, Petra broke her gaze from Phyllis and tromped up the stairs to get her fall cloak. Phyllis could tell her what to do, perhaps, but Petra would be damned if she'd allow the old bat to tell her how to do it.

Ten minutes later, Petra made her way down the narrow path that curled around the woods. Once she was out of sight of the house, she angled away from the path, striding quickly through the tall grass and entering the shadow of the trees. Her anger followed her like a storm cloud, leaving a perceptible pall of coldness in her wake. The rage was so huge and seamless that Petra was hardly even aware of it.

She passed the cairns of her parents' monuments without a glance, stalking directly up to a very large and gnarled tree. It was a singularly ugly tree, twisted, half dead, wearing a partial coat of ragged bark over its bony white trunk. One side of the trunk was covered in thick reddish ivy. Petra already had her wand out. As she stopped in front of the tree, she pointed the wand, drawing it upwards in a slow arc.

The ivy rustled. It unwound itself eerily, creating first a seam, and then a widening gap that spread apart like a stage curtain, revealing a dark space. The trunk of the tree was, in fact, quite hollow, as Petra had long ago discovered. Its inner walls were smooth and dead, its floor carpeted with rotting mulch. Several objects were hidden inside, but Petra ignored most of them. She had come for only one thing, and she reached for it in a businesslike manner. She turned away with the object in her hand, held up in front of her: a broomstick. It was nearly as long as she was tall, with a carefully cropped and threaded tail. The handle was worn smooth. As always, it felt perfectly suited to her hand. As Petra let her gaze move over its length, the ivy behind her knitted shut again, hiding the interior of the hollow tree and the objects within it. The cold pall of Petra's anger settled around her, filling the bowl of the hollow like mist. The air seemed to darken very slightly. Petra smiled slowly, but the smile didn't affect her eyes at all.

Less than a minute later, a dark shape streaked out of the forest, drawing a fan of dead leaves and gritty dust in its wake. It swooped low over the lake, racing its reflection, and then, with a flap of a cloak, it was gone.

Petra leaned over her broom, her teeth bared slightly into the wind, her eyes squinted. She flew low, barely five feet above the snaking line of a stream, matching its curves as it wound through the fields. With the stream's high, rocky banks and bordering trees, it was almost like flying in a natural tunnel. Petra leaned around sharp curves, ducked under fallen trees, and bobbed over sudden marshy outcroppings and boulders. Dragonflies flitted past her, their buzzing barely heard before falling into the distance behind her. It was, in all honesty, extremely dangerous, but Petra didn't care. She touched her chin to the end of her broom, forcing it to go faster, feeling the wild thrash of her hair and the snap of her cloak as she flew. By following the stream into town she was taking the long way, but by flying she was still cutting hours of travel time from her trip. Even so, Petra knew that that wasn't the real reason she'd decided to fly, in spite of Phyllis' orders. She'd done it partly just to defy Phyllis, of course, but that was only a small part of it. Deep down, it was as if Petra was trying to outrun something. Perhaps it was her rage that she was trying to leave behind, or perhaps it was the phantom voice in the back rooms of her mind. Petra had always made a point of trying to be honest with herself, and she knew that the voice had, in fact, been unusually quiet ever since yesterday. What Petra was really trying to outrun was the realization of what had occurred yesterday at the end of the dock, when she'd sent the dead spiders into the water.

She'd thought it had all been over—that it had ended with her final school year. She'd made the right choice, chosen good over her own deepest desires. That choice had left her feeling utterly empty and forlorn, and yet, at the very least, she took some comfort in the knowledge that the nightmare was over, and that she had done the right thing. It was sad to know that she'd never again see her parents' faces, even in the pool's ghostly reflection, but it was also sort of freeing. It was over. She could try to move on.

But that had changed, now. Her mother had appeared once more, teasingly, barely visible in the rippling waters of the lake. This time, it hadn't required any outside magic or malevolent, manipulating force. No one was controlling her or tempting her. Apparently, Petra had conjured that ephemeral image of her dead mother entirely on her own. She didn't know how it was possible. Perhaps she had always had the power, but had never known how to summon it until her encounters with the horrible being called the Gatekeeper. Perhaps she had even somehow learned the skill from that entity, picked it up like osmosis, without even trying. It didn't matter, really. The power to summon the image of her parents was there, inside her. That, in itself, was not what Petra was really fleeing

*She flew low, barely five feet above the snaking line of a stream,
matching its curves as it wound through the fields.*

from. It was the suspicion that that wasn't where her powers ended. The Gatekeeper's ultimate promise had been far more than just allowing Petra fleeting glimpses of her dead parents; the Gatekeeper's promise had been their restoration to her.

That was impossible, of course. Looking back, Petra doubted that even an entity as powerful as the Gatekeeper, whose origin was outside of time and space, whose domain was the Void between the worlds of the living and the dead, could truly restore her lost loved ones to life. But what if it *wasn't* impossible? Even if there was only one chance in a hundred—one chance in a *million*—was it a chance that could be turned down? That's what had propelled Petra throughout her last school year, what had helped her to willingly blind herself to the plots of those who sought to manipulate her. If the promise is tantalizing enough, the odds cease to matter; any chance is a chance worth fighting for, or even dying for. If the promise is great enough, it is worth almost any cost.

*Almost.*

And that was why Petra had chosen to turn it down in the end, hadn't she? Because the Gatekeeper had asked her to do the one thing she couldn't do: kill an innocent person. She'd made the right choice. She'd taken the side of good.

And as Petra thought this, racing along over the arcing stream, flitting in and out of sunlight and shade, golden warmth and autumn chill, the voice in the backrooms of her mind suddenly spoke up again. *Did you really?* It said. *Did you really choose to side with good?*

The squint smoothed out of Petra's eyes as she flew. Of course she'd chosen good. She had decided not to kill. She had saved the girl who was intended to be her victim. She had destroyed the source of the manipulations that had tricked her.

*You did those things,* the voice admitted. *But did you really* choose *them? After all, there* had *been another factor. There had been the boy.*

Yes, Petra recalled. James, her friend. He had come at the last moment. He had revealed the source of those who'd manipulated her, showed her its reality and its shocking ugliness. He had shocked her to her senses just in time.

*Did he?* The voice asked. *Perhaps. But perhaps not. Perhaps he had simply been another manipulation, but only in the opposite direction.*

Another manipulation? Petra had never thought of it that way. It made a strange kind of sense, though. If James had never arrived, she might not have chosen to save the girl in the end. She might indeed have killed her. And if she had, she, Petra, might be in a very different place today, wouldn't she?

The voice spoke reasonably, echoing out of the back of her mind. *It matters not where you would be now. Perhaps the Gatekeeper could have kept its promise to you; after all, you saw your mother standing on the edge of the pool, didn't you? But then again, perhaps not. You may never know. But you do know one thing: you did not make that choice. You were interrupted. You were influenced. In the end, you were manipulated by the boy James, in no less a way than you might have been by the Gatekeeper. You can never know what choice you'd have made on your own. Or what the outcome of that choice might have been.*

It was true. It was a small thing, and yet, in a way, it was monumental. It changed everything. Part of Petra had hated the choice she'd made, but she had at least taken comfort in knowing it had been her choice, one that defined her, made her good, despite the lurking evil she felt moving inside her sometimes. It had proved to her that she could defy that evil; that she could contain it. But what if it hadn't truly been her choice? What if the voice was right? What if she'd merely been manipulated in the opposite direction? If so, then it hadn't even been a choice at all, much less a defining moment.

And now, what if she was being given the chance to make that choice all over again, but with no outside manipulations? *What if?*

Petra blinked and looked around. Without realizing it, she had drifted to a complete stop. She hovered on her broomstick, floating in mid-air over her own rippling reflection. The stream babbled all around her, obliviously. Her hair hung limply against her cheeks. She listened.

Once again, the voice in the back room of her mind had gone silent.

Three hours later, Petra walked along the path leading to the house. The sun was a bright diamond in the cloudless dome of the sky, having transformed the misty morning into a still, humid afternoon. Petra had hidden her broom back inside the hollow tree and now walked brazenly toward the house with her cloak slung over her shoulder, her wind-swept hair pulled back into a loose ponytail.

As it turned out, Mr. Thurman, owner of Thurman's Thrifts and Trade, had indeed granted the Morgansterns credit for a small but sturdy used trunk. Earlier in the summer, Petra had realized that the lifelong bachelor bore a rather quaint older-man's crush on her, although he was far too timid ever to mention it. The idea of using Mr. Thurman's affections as a bargaining tool was vaguely disgusting to Petra, and yet she'd decided that she wanted to prove to Phyllis that she had not, in fact, sent Petra on merely a useless errand. It hadn't taken much. She'd merely engaged Mr. Thurman in some banter about the beauty of the autumn afternoon and how much she loved wildflowers, smiling mistily and wide-eyed at the older man. By the time she mentioned the business of Izzy's trunk, Mr. Thurman was rather red-cheeked. He offered the trunk on credit before Petra had even had to ask for it. She promised that grandfather Warren would be around to pick the trunk up the next day and wished Mr. Thurman a good afternoon. She felt a bit guilty about how easy it had been to get what she wanted from Mr. Thurman, but only a little bit. She skipped as she made her way back to the stream where she had hidden her broomstick.

She was nearly two hours early in returning from the market, but Petra knew that Phyllis wouldn't say anything about it. After all, Mr. Sunnyton's white truck was still leaning slightly in the rutted drive next to the house; the "interview" with Izzy was still in progress. Phyllis would no sooner mention magic in Mr. Sunnyton's presence than break wind, and for the same reasons. With that knowledge seated firmly in Petra's mind, she strode into the shadow of the porch. She reached for the door, and then froze in place.

Voices were raised inside. They echoed down the hall and through the screen door. The first thing Petra heard was Izzy sobbing.

"She's rather young and sickly," a man's voice said over the sound of Izzy's crying. "And a touch, ahem, excitable."

"She's not at all," Phyllis stated flatly, as if it was an order to Izzy. "She's perfectly suited to the work farm. Why, it's all she talks about of late."

Izzy drew a hitching breath. Struggling to control her voice, she said, "I changed my mind. I don't want to go. I want to stay home with you and Papa Warren. I'm not ready yet."

"Nonsense," Phyllis barked. "Mr. Sunnyton is offering you a golden opportunity. If the farm needs you now, then you'll go with him today and I'll hear no more about it. After all, there's no point in your scampering around here for a week if there's an opening for you at the work farm now. Warren will bring your things along presently."

Through the mesh of the screen door, Petra could make out the figure of Percival Sunnyton standing in the entry of the parlor, his back to Petra. He was short and dumpy, though nattily dressed in a white coat and hat. His hands were stuffed in his trouser pockets as he rocked impatiently on his heels. He made a show of looking at his watch.

"Really, perhaps this isn't a good time," he drawled. "There's no need for the girl to come along today if she isn't prepared. There will probably be more openings next year if the girl is unable to attend now."

"That won't be necessary," Phyllis declared coldly, and Petra knew she was staring at Izzy with that steely, implacable gaze, ordering her to silence. This time, however, the gaze didn't work. Apparently, Izzy hadn't truly understood what life at the work farm would be like until she'd seen the impersonal glare of this pudgy, beady-eyed man with the deceptively friendly-sounding name. In a rare display of defiance, Izzy raised her voice.

"But I don't want to!" she wailed. "I'm afraid to go! Don't make me, Mother!"

Phyllis decided on a different tactic. She clucked her tongue dismissively and spoke to the man in the white coat and hat. "She's stubborn, as you can see, but that's what will make her such a good worker. Once she gets to your farm, why, she'll never want to leave." She laughed a little, as if sharing a joke.

"No!" Izzy shouted, now fully committed to her last resort of outright defiance. "I won't go, and you can't make me!"

"That's *enough* of that!" Phyllis commanded, her voice ringing like a hammer on iron. There was a resounding *smack*, followed by a rattle of unsteady footsteps. The tiny *whump* Petra heard was the sound of Izzy's bottom falling hard onto the parlor sofa. Mr. Sunnyton looked away— not out of horror, but out of a sort of distracted propriety, as if he was allowing Phyllis some polite privacy while she tended to necessary business.

Petra was through the door and stalking down the hall before she even knew what she intended to do. By the time the screen door clapped shut behind her, she had pushed past the dumpy man and approached Phyllis, her eyes blazing. Phyllis barely blinked, but her eyes darted downward for a fleeting second. *She's checking to see if my wand is in my hand,* Petra thought. And in fact, it was; the shaft of wood protruded purposefully from her fist, pointing at the floor. She hadn't even been aware of taking it out of her pocket.

"I'm back, *Mother,*" Petra growled, speaking through gritted teeth, turning the last word into an epithet. "Just in time, it seems."

Without taking her gaze from Phyllis, Petra held her left hand out to Izzy, who was sitting rather dazedly on the sofa, one hand to her cheek.

"So you are," Phyllis replied, gathering herself. "And rudely interrupting business you have no stake in. Why don't you be a good girl and make Mr. Sunnyton some tea."

"Er!" Sunnyton blurted nervously. "Er, no! No, thank you, that won't be—"

"I don't think Izzy is ready to go today," Petra said slowly, fingering her wand in her right hand, her left still held out to Izzy.

Phyllis' lips nearly disappeared as her face hardened. "I don't think that's for *you* to decide."

"No it isn't," Petra replied evenly, narrowing her eyes. "It's Izzy's decision. And I believe she already made it."

"Look," Sunnyton interjected, backing through the parlor door. "I'll leave this for you ladies to decide. Feel free to call—"

"Izabella is coming now," Phyllis declared, seething. Sunnyton stopped helplessly in the doorway, obviously at a loss. Phyllis continued, not breaking her gaze away from Petra's eyes. "She doesn't know what's best for her. She's dim. Why, without her *mother* to make such decisions for her, she'd be completely worthless."

Despite how it appeared, Petra was trying very hard to control her anger. It was a difficult task, enough to require almost all of her concentration. Her wand seemed to vibrate in her hand. Behind her, Percival Sunnyton shivered. The room seemed to be suddenly growing quite cold. His breath puffed from his nose in a white vapor. He edged closer to the hall. Petra couldn't bring herself to speak. Instead, she broke away from Phyllis' steely gaze and looked down at Izzy. Izzy merely looked at Petra's outstretched hand, her own small hand still clutched to the cheek Phyllis had struck.

"Come with me, Izzy," Petra said evenly. "Let's go… *scamper* a bit."

"She'll do *no such thing!*" Phyllis commanded, her voice nearly vibrating. She moved to step between Izzy and Petra. The air went grey around them. Fronds of frost unfurled on the corners of the parlor window, spreading with lightning speed. Petra's wand shivered in her hand. Phyllis seemed unaware of the change in the atmosphere of the room. Her face had gone pale, with livid red spots high on her cheeks. She raised her arm to knock Petra's outstretched hand aside. Sunnyton gasped, as if to call a warning, but no words came out. Petra was certain that she wouldn't be able to control her response if Phyllis touched her.

And then another voice spoke from the doorway, freezing Phyllis in place. Petra's heart leapt at the sound of it. It was Grandfather Warren.

"If the girl isn't ready to go, then she doesn't have to," he said. His voice was neither loud nor commanding, and yet it carried a certain grave weight. Petra couldn't recall her Grandfather ever speaking with such quiet ferocity.

Phyllis' eyes darted in his direction, her brow shooting up. In the doorway, Percival Sunnyton turned quickly, looking up at the taller, older man behind him.

"Ah-hah!" the dumpy man forced laughter. "You must be the girl's guardian, Mr. Morganstern! Yes, yes, how right you are! We have no desire to pressure the young lady in any way! I'll just be on my way and look forward to seeing her upon the next week, assuming we still have an arrangement. I'll see myself to the door, thank you, and good afternoon!"

Sunnyton's last few words echoed from the porch as he virtually fled the house, holding his white hat to his head as if some capricious ghost was trying to steal it. A moment later, the engine of his white truck roared to life and he backed swiftly along the drive, slewing anxiously from side to side. No one in the parlor had moved. Petra looked down at the wand in her hand. It was still pointed at the floor; on the rug next to Petra's right foot, a small black starburst smoked faintly.

"She was going to make me go with that man!" Izzy proclaimed, tears still drying on her cheeks. She and Petra had left the house shortly after the fracas, leaving Grandfather Warren and Phyllis staring icily at each other across the parlor. Petra strode purposely into the afternoon haze, propelled by her anger, simply creating as much distance as she could. Izzy trotted to keep up, still firmly holding Petra's hand, her cheeks flushed. The girl's attitude about the "interview" seemed to swing from wounded sadness to tentative anger. Petra had never heard Izzy talk this way.

"How could Mother do that to me? She wasn't even listening! She barely knows that horrible man at all, but she was going to make me go in his truck with him! And you know what else? I wasn't going to be able to come home for the weekends at all! Mother says that it'd be best for me to start thinking of the work farm as my home! She said it'd be easier if I only came back once a month! And she says I can't even take my dolls! What will they do without me? They *need* me!"

"It'll be all right, Iz," Petra said automatically, barely hearing herself.

"No, it won't!" Izzy suddenly cried, yanking her hand out of Petra's and stopping to glare at her. "You didn't hear what they said in there! Even if I don't have to leave today, I'll still have to go there next week! I'm starting to think Mother doesn't even *care* if I'm not here anymore! I'm starting to think—"

Izzy stopped abruptly and tears appeared in her eyes, immediately welling over her cheeks. She pressed her lips together hard, trying to stop them from trembling.

Petra dropped to one knee on the path, drawing the younger girl into an embrace, hating herself for offering such hollow comfort. "Sh-shh," she said into the girl's hair.

Izzy pushed away though, tears running freely down her cheeks. She looked at Petra's shoulder, apparently determined to face a truth she'd been denying for years. "I'm starting to think... that Mother won't even miss me..." Her voice hitched as she sobbed, but she squeezed her eyes shut, forcing herself to go on, to finish the thought. "I don't think she even cares. I think that she *wants* me to be gone."

Finally, she collapsed against Petra again and allowed the older girl to hold her. Izzy cried; huge, brokenhearted sobs that broke on Petra's shoulder like ocean waves. Petra simply held her and stroked her hair. She'd always assumed Izzy had been utterly unaware of her own mother's disdain for her, but now she saw that the girl had known all along, deep down, in the secret burial chamber of her young heart. Izzy had been able to deceive herself about her mother for eleven years, but today that deception had collapsed. Phyllis had knocked down that carefully laid falsehood with her own hand. It had been easy. It had only taken one slap. It hadn't been much of a slap, really; the mark on Izzy's cheek had already faded away. But it had been enough, and somehow Petra knew that, for Izzy, there was no going back.

"If I was a witch, this would be easier," Izzy suddenly blurted against Petra's shoulder, her breath hot and fierce. "If I was a witch, I could change things. I could make myself smart. I could make Mother love me. But I'm not a witch. I'm not even a true Muddle. I'm a Wuddle."

Izzy pushed away from Petra again and looked out over the grassy hilltop, her eyes thick with tears. "I'm just a Wuddle. I'm caught right in the middle and I can't do *any*thing right. Maybe Mother's right. Maybe I *am* worthless. Maybe it'd be better for everybody if I just went away forever. Forever and ever."

Petra looked out across the hilltop, following Izzy's gaze. There, standing sentinel-like at the top of the hill was the lone tree in Grandfather's field; the tree Izzy always called the Wishing Tree.

"What are you doing, Izzy?" Petra asked, her voice barely a whisper.

Izzy answered simply, her voice even, her eyes unmoving from that huge, twisted tree. "I'm wishing," she said, her small face pale and grave. "That's all. I'm just wishing."

# *Three*

Late that night, for the first time in years, Petra snuck out of the house. She inched the screen door closed behind her and moved lightly across the porch, stepping over the creakiest planks. She didn't need to sneak anymore, really. Part of her knew that. She could keep the planks from creaking or the screen door from squeaking merely by thinking about it, if she wished. In fact, if she so desired, she could simply place Phyllis and her grandfather into a sleep so deep that they'd not hear a marching band in the upstairs hall, much less her midnight wanderings. But Petra didn't do any of those things. Sneaking out was part of the ritual. In some strange way, sneaking was part of what had always made it work.

When her bare feet hit the dewy grass below the porch, Petra drew a deep breath of cool night air. The moon was merely a bony sliver, riding low in the sky over the nearby woods. Silently, Petra set out toward it, ignoring the path and cutting straight across the garden toward the woods. She'd done this so many times over the years that it was a wonder she hadn't worn her own path. Her feet were wet with dew by the time she entered the arms of the forest and began the descent to the hollow. Crickets chirred all around her, making a long, ringing note in the dark air.

The hollow opened before her, as it always did. Moonlight filtered down through the trees, making shifting patterns on the cairns of her parents. As always, the silvery moonlight and the still of the hollow made Petra think of an underwater scene, a magical Atlantis setting full of whimsy and solemnity. Petra made her way slowly around the cairns. When she reached the old fallen tree however, she did not sit on it. She stood and stared at the cairns, her eyes bright and empty. She had intended to talk to the graves, as she had when she'd been young. Now that she was here, however, she couldn't do it. For the first time in her life, the graves didn't seem like graves at all. They were simply piles of stones. Monuments, yes, but not to her dead parents. As Petra looked at them, it occurred to her that they were, instead, monuments to two girls—the young Petra, who had built them, and Izzy, whose innocence had been killed by a single smack from her mother's hand. The cairns were the graves of Petra's and Izzy's youth. Maybe that had always been their purpose, even when Petra had first built them. Maybe she only saw it now because now, tonight, both graves were finally filled. It was sad, but Petra did not cry. Youth always ends, eventually. Maybe, in a sense, one can only begin to grow when it does. Maybe life only truly begins to happen when innocence dies.

A subtle breeze blew through the hollow, whispering through the turning leaves and rustling the vines knotted over the cairns. Once again, the scene looked like an underwater vista, full of blue depth and eternal silence.

Petra turned away from the cairns. Behind her, the old hollow tree creaked in the breeze, calling her. She walked toward it, producing her wand. She drew it upwards, as if drawing a vertical line in the night air. The vines that embraced the tree spread apart again, whispering to themselves. As a child, Petra had been able to do that without a wand, merely by thinking it. She longed for that simple, effortless power again. The wand was a crutch, imposed on her by a weaker magical world. Part of her resented it deeply. She wanted to be able to do magic the way she used to—without a wand or a word. Perhaps someday she'd master that ability again. She'd make an effort to practice it, to try to find those secret mental muscles again. Those powers had to be there still, if only she looked for them, tried once again to flex them.

She entered the darkness of the hollow tree. Her broom leaned in the shadows, but Petra ignored it. Instead, she knelt and placed her hands on either side of a small box, rather like a jewelry case. It was made of black wood, polished to a mirror-like shine. It felt very cool in her hands. She held it before her as she stood. Leaves crunched under her feet as she carried it out of the hollow tree.

Petra didn't open the box as she walked, climbing the gentle slope out of the hollow. She already knew what was in it, although she didn't understand it. It was ugly, cold, and yet, in some mad, unknowable way, comforting. Even now, just holding the box, it felt right. Not *good*, exactly. In a sense, holding the box felt anything *but* good. But it felt right. *Complete*, somehow.

The trees thinned as Petra reached the edge of the woods, and she wasn't at all surprised to see the glittering surface of the lake spread ahead of her. She had walked all the way through the band of woods, coming out on the far side. Ahead of her, the dock stretched out like a dark omen, pointing inexplicably at nothing. The lake mirrored the blue of the night sky, cut in half by a stripe of dancing reflected moonlight. Petra didn't break her stride. She carried the box out onto the dock, tucking it under her arm as she went. The worn planks were still warm from the past day's sun. They dried the soles of Petra's bare feet as she walked to the end of the dock.

Carefully, Petra squatted and set the black box on the planks behind her. As she straightened, she took her wand from the pocket of her night dress.

She sighed deeply, and it turned into a violent shudder. She didn't want to do it, but she had to know for sure. Closing her eyes, she cast her mind back out over the farm. This was another skill she had almost lost to her childhood. If she concentrated, even now, she could envision the entire farm in her mind, like a sculpture. There was the sleeping house and the darkened barn with Bethel inside, awake, chewing her cud. There was the neat furrowed expanse of Grandfather Warren's field, the Wishing Tree, the piles of rocks. There was the dew beaded grass of the garden, full of the tiny lives of the spiders and squirrels. And then, finally, Petra found what she was searching for. In her mind, she saw the small chicken yard and the ramshackle coop. There were the tiny blue candles of the sleeping chickens… and then there was a brighter candle, an insistent green flicker: a fox. Petra had heard Grandfather Warren talking about the fox. It had been taking one or two chickens a month throughout the summer, although Grandfather had not determined how it was getting past the chicken fence. Petra could see it now: there was a shallow burrow dug under the rear corner, hidden in a patch of heather. The fox could scuttle through, barely fitting, and nab the chicken nearest to the coop door, clamping its narrow jaws on the chicken's sleeping neck before she gave the slightest squawk of alarm. In her mind, Petra could see the fox, crouched low on its haunches, backing through the shallow burrow, dragging the dead chicken after it. Its eyes were bright and beady, and Petra couldn't help thinking of the beady, soulless stare of Percival Sunnyton.

Petra concentrated on the bright green flicker of the fox's mind. She called it. The fox didn't want to come—it wanted to slink off into the woods and enjoy its kill in private. But Petra was insistent. In her mind, she felt the fox resist, saw it drop the dead chicken and snap the air around its head, as if it could bite at her invisible hand.

*More chickens,* Petra said to the fox's mind. *Fat chickens, all the chickens you want. But you must come now, quickly; you must hurry.* The fox hesitated for a moment on the edge of indecision, but then its greed got the better of it. It darted off into the tall grass with a flash of its orange tail, leaving its kill wedged under the wire fence.

Half a minute later, Petra heard the noise of its approach. It rustled eagerly through the weeds, its pelt now ratty with dew. She turned as its claws clittered onto the base of the dock. It saw her and suddenly scrambled to a stop. Its eyes caught the moonlight greenly, making two bright pinpricks in the darkness. Petra could see its black lips drawn back in a snarl. Its whiskers were speckled with blood.

*Come,* Petra told the fox's mind. This close up, Petra had a good glimpse of the creature's mean little soul. It was mad and hungry and greedy, full of the bloodlust of its recent kill. Amazingly, in its palpitating, racing thoughts, it saw Petra not as a threat, but as a fresh victim. It began to creep down the dock toward its captive prize, lifting its black-gloved feet slowly, stalking. It purred a long, ragged growl as it approached.

Petra's wand was still in her hand. She'd assumed she'd feel badly about doing this, but now that she saw the creature, smelled the blood on its dripping, narrow muzzle, she didn't feel bad at all. The fox saw her raise her arm. Its eyes brightened and its jaws opened. It crouched to pounce. A flash of bright green lit the dock the moment it leapt and the life snuffed out of the fox even as it soared through the air, jaws unhinged for the kill.

It tumbled awkwardly at Petra's feet instead, a pile of orange fur and white, bloody teeth. Petra gasped, suddenly horrified at what she'd done. She covered her mouth with her hand, her eyes wide, reflecting the starry sky.

*It was a rodent,* the voice in the back of her mind suddenly stated. *Grandfather will be pleased that you killed it. He would have done it himself if he'd been able. It showed no mercy to its victims, and it deserved none from you.*

There was something essentially wrong with the voice's logic, but Petra couldn't pinpoint it. More importantly, she didn't want to. The fox was dead, but the deed was not yet complete. Still shuddering at what she had done, Petra knelt. She grasped the fox's ratty tail gingerly in her left hand. The body was surprisingly light when she lifted it. She turned around on her knees, shivering now in the cold of the night, and held the dead fox out over the black water.

She drew a shuddering breath and let go. The small body barely made a splash as it hit the surface of the lake. It floated for a moment as the fur soaked into the water, and then, slowly, it began to sink.

"I did it," Petra suddenly said, and the shiver in her voice made it sound as if she was laughing. "I killed, just like I was supposed to. I paid the price, just to see you Mum! Can I see you? I need to talk to you. I really need a Mum now." She did laugh this time, raggedly, at the absurd understatement of it all. A tear ran down her nose and plopped into the lake, following the fox's carcass. "Where are you? Show me, please... I paid the price. Blood for blood. Show me, Mum. Talk to me!"

The rippling water lapped lightly at the pilings of the dock. The sliver of moon danced on its surface.

Slowly, Petra climbed to her feet. There was nothing there. No face looking up at her from the depths. No comforting smile. Nothing but mute water and dead reflections. Petra didn't think it was still possible, but her heart broke. She hitched a sob and raised her eyes from the dark waves below the dock.

And saw the figure standing in the water in the middle of the lake.

Petra's sob turned into a violent gasp of surprise and she clapped both hands to her mouth. This was no reflection. The figure stood in the middle of the lake's mirror-like surface, silhouetted against that glittering stripe of moonlight. It was a woman, of course. Petra couldn't make out any features, and yet she recognized the shape from her visions in the chamber of the pool; it was her mother. Waves lapped against her waist where she stood in the water, her arms at her sides, her head cocked slightly, watching. Her hair wasn't even wet.

"Mum!" Petra tried to cry, but it came out as merely a strangled, hoarse whisper. She was simultaneously terrified and exultant. She forced breath into her lungs. "I did it, Mum! Blood for blood! I did it!"

Tears ran freely down Petra's cheeks as she stood on the edge of the dock, smiling, her arms held out to the shape across the water. "I don't know what to do, Mum," Petra called, her voice shaking. "Izzy and Phyllis and Grandfather Warren... it's all so confusing and messy. I know I'm supposed to help, somehow. That's why I came back, I think. But I just don't know how! I'm lost, Mum! And I'm afraid! What should I do?"

Across the waves, the figure shook her head slowly. Petra understood it not as a statement of ignorance, but of helplessness. Her mother wanted to help, but she couldn't. She was held back, somehow. She couldn't approach her daughter, or even make herself heard. Petra noticed that the water was up to her mother's chest now. She was sinking again.

"No!" Petra cried, inching forward on the dock so that her toes curled over the edge. "Mum! Don't go already! I need you! I've always needed you! Tell me what to do! Tell me... tell me you love me and it'll be all right!"

The grief roared through Petra, fresh and new, as if she was losing her mother all over again. She moaned and sobbed at the same time. Across the water, her mother held her arms out, reaching toward Petra, trying to offer what little comfort she could. The water sucked her in, wetting the sleeves of her dress, washing over her shoulders.

*The figure stood in the middle of the lake's mirror-like surface,
silhouetted against the glittering stripe of moonlight.*

"NOOO!" Petra cried hoarsely. She nearly jumped into the water herself, momentarily forgetting the deadly tangle of the sunken gazebo. She looked at the sinking silhouette through her own outstretched fingers, as if she meant to pluck the shape from the water by sheer force of will. She couldn't do it, and even as she watched, the shape of her mother dipped finally into the glimmering band of moonlight, swallowed away as if she had never been.

Petra stumbled backwards and collapsed into a sitting position on the dock, clapping her hands over her face and sobbing helplessly. The emotions in her were simply too huge to contain. They stormed through her heart as if they might rip her apart. Several minutes went by and the storm of grief and loss finally began to abate.

Petra slowly took her hands away from her face and looked with red eyes out over the lake. She felt exhausted, emptied, wrung out like an old washcloth. In the weary emptiness of her thoughts, only one thing remained.

*It had worked.*

Not perfectly, of course. Her mother had not been able to approach her or speak to her, but she had been there. It hadn't been a dream or a vision. Petra could do it again, if she wished, and she could do it better. Simply killing an animal wasn't enough. The fox had indeed been a mere rodent, mean and greedy in its own small way. Its blood was tainted, insufficient. But there were other options. Petra explored them in the dark chambers of her mind, cautiously, tentatively. She leaned back on her hands as she mused, her tears still drying in the cool midnight air.

As she leaned back, Petra was aware of the shaft of her wand still held in the loose fist of her right hand. She wasn't aware, however, that her left hand rested on the cool polished wood of the mysterious black box. It glinted mutely in the pale moonlight, keeping its own secrets.

The next few days drifted by in a cold fog, both inside and outside the Morganstern farmhouse. Grey mist hung over the field and the woods, wet and dank, dripping from the turning leaves. Grandfather Warren spent as much time as possible out of the house, leaving very early in the mornings and returning only for meals, usually still wearing his work boots and dirty coveralls. Phyllis moved through the house like a miniature cyclone, stomping and slamming doors as she performed her daily routine. She exuded anger like a stench. Petra knew, however, that unlike herself, Phyllis reveled in anger. It was her natural element. In a way, Phyllis was only truly happy when she had something to be righteously furious about it. Nothing had been said about the confrontation in the parlor during Percival Sunnytons's visit, but Petra knew it wasn't over. Phyllis was merely biding her time. Grandfather knew it, even without his latent ability to read his wife's mind. He was not a strong man—the confrontation that day in the parlor had taken every ounce of his limited resolve and courage—and Phyllis terrified him in a way that no one else could. Petra was ashamed of her Grandfather for that, and yet she knew that it was that very fear that had compelled him to marry the woman in the first place.

Petra's grandmother had always been the ruling force of the Morganstern household. A large woman in every sense of the word, she had been firm, decisive and unapologetically in command. The vacuum her death had created in Grandfather Warren's personal world had been so huge that he simply hadn't known how to operate without her. In a desperate act of wanton self preservation, Grandfather had found Phyllis, herself recently widowed. Phyllis was nearly two decades younger than Warren, mother of a baby girl with special needs and alone in a house she could no longer afford. Despite their obvious differences, they were eerily perfect for each other: Grandfather Warren needed a strong woman to rule him and his household, and Phyllis needed a home and a meek man who would submit to her. Later, it had probably occurred to Warren that he had gotten more than he'd bargained for with Phyllis. Like his first wife, Phyllis was strong, opinionated and commanding; unlike his first wife, however, Phyllis was mean, belittling and petty. Still, Warren revered her. Many times, Petra had thought that Grandfather Warren loved Phyllis in the same way that an African tribal native might love a small, capricious god, one who demands much and gives little, but who promises power if it is ever truly required. It was a twisted love, and it certainly wasn't mutual, but it was apparently the only kind of love Grandfather Warren expected in life.

Petra knew that Phyllis would make Grandfather's life ugly for weeks—her repayment for his interference on the day of Percival Sunnyton's visit. But Grandfather's interference had not really changed anything. Izzy was still scheduled to leave the following Monday morning; Grandfather had even gone to the market and retrieved the small trunk that Petra had negotiated. Phyllis took pleasure in raging at Warren simply because she knew it upset him. The god was displeased, and this meant that the native owed penance. Phyllis was enjoying thinking of ways Warren would have to appease her.

Her anger at Petra, however, was a different thing entirely. Phyllis and Petra understood each other too well to have anything more than a cold relationship at the best of times. Phyllis knew that, unlike

Grandfather Warren, Petra could not be intimidated into submission. The only power Phyllis had over Petra was the girl's love of her Grandfather, and that was barely a toehold, a meager trump card at best. Petra, on the other hand, knew that, under her bluster and threats, Phyllis was afraid of her. Phyllis herself was barely even aware of that fear, but it was there, ticking like a bomb. Phyllis only knew that Petra was a threat to her dominance in the household, and it made her deeply uneasy. She'd always hated the girl, but it had been a cool hate, congealed, expressed only in small degradations and veiled insults. After all, the girl was only temporary. Phyllis had worked carefully and deliberately to make Petra's life as unpleasant as possible, so as to assure the girl's departure from the farm the moment she came of age. And yet, Petra had not left. She had returned, inexplicably, despite the fact that she *had* come of age and graduated from the ridiculous school of witchcraft. Worse, the girl was interfering even more than usual, brazenly and unflinchingly. Petra sensed that Phyllis was plotting against her, calculating how best to be rid of her once and for all. By comparison, Phyllis' anger at Warren was a mere hobby. Phyllis' rage at Petra was a white hot fury, desperate, and at its deepest heart, terrified.

Izzy avoided her mother as much as possible. She had abandoned her attempts to talk Phyllis out of sending her to the work farm. Instead, Izzy had simply resigned herself to her bleak future, and that resignation had taken most of the life out of her. She was listless and uninterested in playing. She had even stopped playing dolls with Petra before nights out.

"You be Astra," Petra had prompted the night before, straightening the hair of the one of Izzy's dolls and handing it to her. "Mr. Bobkins will be Treus, all right? We can do the scene with the Marsh Hag. That's our favorite."

Izzy had taken the doll, but had simply held it in her lap, looking down at it. She sighed. "Mr. Bobkins says he doesn't want to play Treus anymore," she said.

"What do you mean, Iz?" Petra smiled, holding up the small, nappy teddy bear. "He's the only boy in the bunch. He has to play Treus."

Izzy shook her head. "Nobody wants to play anymore. They all told me last night. They told me they were too grown up for playing anymore."

Petra tilted her head ironically. "I'm older than they are, Iz, and *I* still play."

"You only play because of me," Izzy answered, setting her doll on the floor, carefully, in a seated position, its legs sprawled out before it. The doll, Beatrice, flopped forward, staring at the floor between its oversized feet as if in deep thought. Izzy stared at the doll. "But you don't have to anymore, either. Playing isn't fun anymore."

Petra studied the girl who, for all intents and purposes, was her baby sister. "How can playing not be fun anymore?"

Izzy drew a long, deep sigh, and then raised her eyes to Petra's, her face unsmiling, pathetically unguarded. "It's not real, anymore, Petra," she said simply. "It used to be different. It used to be... I don't know...like a dream, maybe, but a dream of something real. A dream that you could think will someday come true."

Petra didn't know what to say. She simply looked at her sister, watching as Izzy looked down and patted Beatrice lightly on the head, as if comforting the doll in its deep, troubling thoughts. Petra desperately wished she could say something to Izzy, something to bring back that irrepressible sweetness, but nothing came. There were no arguments to be made, because in her heart, Petra knew Izzy was right. She knew exactly what her sister meant.

One the day before Petra's last trip out to the dock, she went up to her room and stood before her window. The ratty curtains were still drawn, cutting the gloomy afternoon light in half so that the room was a cave of shadows. Downstairs, Phyllis stomped and slammed, clanking dishes as she prepared dinner. Petra could see through the dingy lace of the curtains; Izzy was out in the garden, picking the last of the season's berries, staining her fingers in happy colors and occasionally sucking the juice off them, unsmiling. Petra simply watched.

*It can't go on this way.*

The thought came to her from the back room of her mind, but it sounded like her own voice this time. She nodded slightly to herself. It was true. The simmer of Phyllis' anger was still steadily rising, fuelled by her fear of Petra and her desperation to force her out of the household for good. And yet, Petra couldn't just leave. Not yet, not while Izzy still needed her.

*It isn't Izzy you are staying for.*

Again, the voice was her own. Either the voice in the back room of her mind had finally faded away, or it was getting good at disguising itself. The words rang true, though. Izzy wasn't the reason Petra had stayed. Izzy was soon destined for a life of manual labor and drudgery, forced into it by her own hateful mother. Certainly Izzy was not the smartest girl in the world, but she was not hopeless. Her simplicity had, in fact, been beautiful in its way. Petra knew that there were schools for children like Izzy, schools with caring teachers that knew how to teach children who had learning disabilities. Those schools cost money, as Phyllis had once tersely pointed out, putting the subject neatly to rest, but Petra knew better. The money wasn't the issue; Phyllis wouldn't have spent it on Izzy even if she'd had it. Phyllis simply didn't believe Izzy had any potential for school. It was almost as if Phyllis blamed her daughter for being born the way she had, and intended to punish her for it. As far as she was concerned, the work farm provided the only real option for the girl. Thus, in less than two days, Izzy would be sent away, most likely for the rest of her life. Izzy no longer needed Petra to defend her and look out for her. In fact, if that had been Petra's task, she had failed miserably at it.

*It can't go on this way.*

Petra sighed shallowly. Finally, she turned her back to the window and walked across the room. She knelt and drew something out from under her bed. It was the black box from the hollow tree. It felt heavy in her hands as she lifted it and placed it on the bed. Kneeling there on the floor, she was nearly eye-level with it. The gloomy light of the room glinted on the polished lid.

Petra opened it.

She knew what was in it, and yet the sight of it always made her shiver. She didn't know why. She didn't know where the object had come from or whose it had been. She'd simply discovered it in the hollow tree when she'd come home from school for the last time. Somehow she knew that the box hadn't been placed there by any living soul. No one knew of her hiding place, and she could tell it had not been discovered or disturbed. The box had simply found its way there. The box, or rather the object *in* the box, had known it might be needed. It had simply gone to its mistress, hiding away where it knew only she would find it.

The object in the box collected the dim light of the room, glinting wickedly. It was a dagger. Its blade was tarnished black, almost as if it had been rubbed with soot. The handle was singularly ugly, encrusted with jewels.

Almost daintily, Petra wrapped her fingers around the handle and lifted it. If holding the black box felt right, then touching the dagger itself felt positively electric. It was like holding a live viper, or the very tide of the oceans. It felt powerful and dangerous, but mostly it felt like hers. There was very little in the world that belonged to Petra, yet the dagger belonged to her in a way that surpassed mere ownership. It was like a part of her, like she belonged to it as much as it to her. It was a frightening feeling, and yet it was the only thing that comforted her. The dagger spoke without words. It promised things—secret things, perhaps even dark and terrible things, but Petra found herself irresistibly drawn to it.

*If I had parents, I wouldn't need this,* she thought. It was an argument against a warning that no one had voiced. It was an innate defensiveness. Part of her knew that the dagger was evil. But it was also powerful, and it could possibly help her. Would it truly be wrong to use an evil tool to do something good? If it was the only real option available to her, who could blame her for embracing that option?

"I won't need it forever," she said softly to herself and the empty, shadowy room. "I will only use it once. After that, I will put it away. Just this once. That's all. That's all I need."

"Reminds me of something a friend said recently," a voice answered quietly, shocking her. Petra gasped and spun, waving the dagger wildly ahead of her, her eyes wide.

A shape stood in the corner. It was huge, towering in the shadows, indistinct. It was nearly invisible in the dimness of the room.

The figure went on in a deep, rumbling voice. "He told me that those who choose to do good generally get a taste for it. I think that that is true, but I think that it is only half the story. Can you imagine what the other half of that truth is, Miss Morganstern?"

Petra's heart slammed in her chest. She scrambled to get her feet beneath her, pushing herself upright against the bed. She still held the dark dagger in front of her. "Who are you?" she demanded in a hoarse whisper.

The figure stepped forward slightly, moving into the dim light of the room. "I apologize, Miss Morganstern. I don't do this for all of my former students, but I thought you might be worthy of a little personal visit. Call it an academic follow-up."

Petra squinted, finally recognizing the tall man. "Headmaster?" she said, keeping her voice low. "Merlinus? But why?"

Merlinus Ambrosius, figure of legend and the headmaster of the wizarding school Petra had recently graduated from, sighed and spread his hands slightly, glancing down. It was a gesture that seemed to encompass Petra, the dagger, the room and the entire farm, all at once. He sighed. "May I sit down, Miss Morganstern? We have much to discuss."

Petra nodded curtly. She realized she was still holding the dagger tightly, as if for reassurance. Part of her thought she should put it back in the black box, but she couldn't quite bring herself to do it.

Across the room, Merlin settled himself gracefully onto a narrow chair by the window.

Petra allowed herself to sink onto the edge of the bed, where she sat bolt upright. "Does Phyllis know you're here?"

"By 'Phyllis', I assume you mean the rather unhappy woman downstairs. No, most assuredly she does not. But you are aware of that, I think. I am not here to speak to anyone but you."

"Have you been spying on me?"

"I have been watching you, Miss Morganstern," Merlin replied evenly, meeting her eyes. "And for good reason, as you may guess."

Petra swallowed. "Are you going to… to arrest me?"

*Petra felt the weight of his gaze, as if he were looking past her,
into her, balancing the merit of her deepest thoughts and fears.*

Merlin studied her for a long moment. "I have no authority to arrest you, Miss Morganstern. Nor do I wish to, despite the fact that arresting you might well be the wisest course of action. Not because of what you have already done, but because of what you are capable of doing."

Petra didn't know what to say to that. Merlin waited. Finally, in a small voice, she said, "I'm not capable of anything."

Merlin narrowed his eyes consideringly. "In a sense, that is true," he answered quietly. He leaned forward on the small chair. "You have erected a very secure cage for yourself, I think. Very few people are aware of what you can do, and not the least of them is yourself. You have forgotten more magic than some of the most powerful witches and wizards in the world will ever know, and you have done so willingly, deliberately. That has required enormous self control, Miss Morganstern. Frankly, I would not have believed it was possible. And why have you done this? For acceptance. For the hope of love from those too mean or too powerless to give it. The loss of your parents has created in you a longing for acceptance so strong that it has driven you to deny yourself powers that lesser creatures would kill for. Ironically, the same sense of loss and alienation that created the most powerful villain of all time has, in you, created the best safeguard against such corruption. And yet…"

Merlin stopped. Petra felt the weight of his gaze, as if he were looking past her, into her, balancing the merit of her deepest thoughts and fears. It was exquisitely disquieting. She fidgeted and clutched the dagger tighter, trying to hide it from Merlin, even though he'd obviously already seen it.

"And yet even that safeguard may not be enough," Merlin said softly, finishing his thought. "Perhaps no safeguard could be. Perhaps some powers must be willingly confronted rather than caged. What do you think, Miss Morganstern?"

Petra looked away, out the window. She worked to keep her expression blank. "I don't know what you are talking about," she replied, her voice nearly monotone.

"Oh, I believe you do," Merlin said. "You have always tried to be honest with yourself. I admire that. Do so now, my friend. I am no mere wizard, and you are no mere witch. Do not taunt me with feigned ignorance."

Petra glanced back at Merlin, her curiosity piqued, although she tried not to let him see it. "What do you mean, I am no 'mere witch'?"

Merlin sat back again, glancing around the room idly. Raising his eyebrows, he asked, "Pardon me for asking, Miss Morganstern, but where do you keep your wand?"

Petra furrowed her brow slightly. "It's in my dresser," she answered, gesturing with her left hand, the one that wasn't holding the dagger. "Top drawer. Phyllis doesn't like to see it, so I keep it hidden most of the time."

Merlin glanced at the dresser, then, without turning his head, slid his eyes back to Petra. "You'd have no way of knowing this, considering your grandfather's rather sad choice to deny his own wizarding character, but it is extremely rare for any witch or wizard not to carry their wand on their person at all times. For most witches and wizards, the wand is very nearly an extension of the body. Do you find this curious?"

Petra shrugged slightly. After a moment, she said, "What about you? You don't carry your staff all the time. I've noticed."

"This is true," Merlin acknowledged, inclining his head slightly. "And do you know why?"

Petra didn't like the look in Merlin's eye, nor the direction the interview seemed to be taking. Still, she was curious. "You don't carry your staff," she said, meeting the headmaster's gaze, "because you don't need it to do magic."

Merlin smiled very slightly. "In my time, there were those who reviled the very use of wands and staffs. They felt that the use of magical tools was a weakness, that it would eventually breed a dependency on external sources of magic. Of course, even then, it was the exceedingly rare witch or wizard who could perform any real magic without such assistance. Realistically, wands have always been an essential medium for the wizarding world. Without them, the magic is directionless and unfocussed, diluted to uselessness."

Merlin paused again, the smile gone from his face. The gloom of the bedroom was deepening as early evening fell beyond the window. Clouds were rolling in with the night, low and menacing. Petra could barely make out the headmaster's expression in the descending darkness. When he spoke again, Petra could hardly see his lips moving.

"You do not need your wand to perform the magic, do you, Miss Morganstern?"

Petra didn't answer. For some reason, she didn't want to. Merlin waited, unmoving. Finally, she stirred on the bed, moving slightly away from him. "I… of course I do." It wasn't a lie, exactly. She had forgotten that ability. She was no longer able to make the magic happen with only her thoughts. She needed the wand now, just like anyone else.

"How hard was it to learn to rely on your wand, when you first got it?" Merlin asked in his low, rumbling voice. "Did it seem clumsy? Fragile? I imagine it was like trying to force a waterfall through a funnel. I imagine it was very frustrating at first—like you were limiting yourself, killing a part of your very being. Was it like that? Tell me, Miss Morganstern. I am quite curious."

Petra narrowed her eyes. The dagger hummed silently in her hand. She pressed her lips together, suddenly feeling a surge of anger. And then, strangely, it was gone. She felt preternaturally calm.

"I remember the first time," she whispered, staring out the window at the grey, advancing clouds. "I was eleven. Grandfather Warren had taken me to a small wand shop in an alley in Devonshire. The shop was actually a shoe store, but the owner was a wizard named Rufus; he sold wands out of a dark little room in the back of the store. He smelled like leather and his hands were very rough. He had arthritis. I could see it, like steel wool bunched in his knuckles. I could have fixed it, but I didn't know him, and he scared me a little. He had lots of narrow boxes stacked on shelves. After he looked at me for a minute, he pulled one of the boxes out and took a wand from it. He put the wand in my hand and asked me how it felt. I told him. I told him it felt like a stick from the tree in grandfather's field. He laughed and told me to give it a flick."

Petra looked at Merlin before going on. "Nothing happened. Nothing at all. No flash, no sparkles, nothing. But the wand had broken. When I handed it back to the store owner, it had cracked all the way along its length. It fell into two pieces in his hand. I hadn't just broken it; I'd killed it. It was too small." Petra sighed deeply and looked out the window again. "We left with a wand that night, but I hadn't tried it out. The store owner hadn't suggested that I test any more of his wands. He just sold Grandfather one that looked about right and sent us on our way. I learned to use it, but only because I started small. I learned to manage how much magic I sent through it. It was the only way. And then, eventually, I wasn't even aware of holding back. After awhile, my magic seemed to adjust to it, and I got used to the wand. I forgot how *not* to use it. It's just like the people in your day said, isn't it? I got dependent on the tool."

Merlin remained impassive in his posture, but his voice was low and tense. "You don't know, do you? You now know that, due to the evil schemes of wicked men, your very soul is tainted with the last shred of the most evil wizard in the world. And yet, even still, you think that your experience with the wand is not uncommon among young witches and wizards. You believe your experience is unusual, but not extraordinary. Is this not so?"

Petra looked at the dark shape. She did think that. How could it be otherwise? She nodded slowly.

"I *prefer* my staff, Miss Morganstern," Merlin said meaningfully. "It has traveled with me long and served me well. It is comfortable to me. And yet, I do not *need* it. Do you know why this is?"

Petra didn't answer. She simply stared at the dark shape of the big man, her eyes wide and expressionless. In her hand, the dagger hummed.

"It is because I am not a wizard," Merlin said softly. "I am a *sorcerer*. A sorcerer's magic is quite different. It comes not only from within himself, but from the world all around. A sorcerer can tap into the enormous magic of the world at large, shape it and wield it. This is the true basis of his power, and the meaning of his title, for the main difference between a wizard and a sorcerer *is* the source. I had believed I was the last sorcerer, and in a sense, I was right. But only in a sense."

Petra simply stared. Did Merlin mean what it sounded like he was saying? Her thoughts raced, replaying her life. She saw herself as a child, mentally levitating the dishes from the table to the sink, closing the parlor curtains with her thoughts only, since she was too short to reach the cord. She saw herself in the cellar, terrified, finding the tiny spark of life in the horrible rats, snuffing them out one by one, shuddering at the sight of their curled bodies. Mostly, she saw the look of fear on her grandmother's face as she took the switch off the poplar tree, swatting it smartly across young Petra's knuckles, once for each dead rat. It was that look that had followed her through her childhood, that look of restrained terror that had so shamed and haunted Petra, even to this day.

"I'm not a witch," Petra said, her voice barely above a whisper.

In the darkness, Merlin shook his head slowly. "You are not a witch," he concurred.

Petra looked at the dark figure, her eyes imploring. "But what am I, then?"

"You are a sorceress," Merlin answered, telling her what she now knew. "The only living sorceress in the earth, perhaps for as long as a thousand years. I do not know how this came to be so. The origins of sorcerers and sorceresses are famously difficult to trace, but the most common explanation is that they are the seventh children of seventh children. This is obviously not the case for you, Miss Morganstern. Similarly, legend says that a sorcerer or sorceress shall appear in the earth only when the balance of magic requires it. It may well be that this is currently the case, although I have not been able to divine the details of that balance. The point is that you are what you are. And more importantly, this is true of you *despite* what occurred to you during your last school term."

Petra remembered: the pool with the reflections of her parents; the Gatekeeper and its promise of their return; the night when she almost fulfilled the bargain, almost committed the murder of a young girl, believing that it was the price she must pay to bring her lost parents back. "You mean, the Gatekeeper didn't know I was... what I am? It thought I was just a regular witch?"

"I do not claim to know what the Gatekeeper knew," Merlin replied. "But I am willing to wager that its earthly cohorts did not know you were a sorceress, even when they cursed you with the unfortunate destiny of carrying the last ghostly vestige of their fallen lord. All of this, you might choose to believe, is either a fantastic coincidence, or it is part of a destiny far greater than we can currently comprehend."

"But why me?" Petra suddenly asked, the force of the words surprising even herself. "Why my parents? What did any of us do to get the attention of destiny in such a big way? I don't *want* this!"

Merlin nodded. "I sympathize, Miss Morganstern. And yet, I suspect even in your youth you understand the futility of asking why things like this happen. Such questions may form the livelihood of scholars and philosophers, but they are empty words to people such as us.

You do not have the luxury of merely railing against the unfortunate nature of your identity. Your task, as I think you understand, is clear."

Petra felt the helpless anger rising inside her again. In the darkness, her eyes glinted like coins. "Tell me," she said flatly.

Merlin's face was inscrutable in the darkness. "Your task is to maintain the cage you have so far created."

"Maintain it?" Petra exclaimed, shocked. "You can't mean that!"

"Indeed I do, and you know why this must be so," Merlin replied evenly. "One of the wisest things ever said is this: to whom much is given, much is required. Much has been given to you, Miss Morganstern. You asked for none of it, and yet the fact remains: you are more significant than you can possibly know. Your power is terrible, and you have only begun to learn to control it. The day may come when you must give vent to that power, but until then, your duty—grave and monstrous as it is—is not to let it control you. For once you give it voice, it will rule you. Far lesser powers have destroyed witches and wizards far stronger than you are. Learn from their mistakes, Miss Morganstern. For if you do not..."

Merlin stopped again, allowing his words to hang in the air, ringing with unspoken tension.

Petra slowly narrowed her eyes. Very quietly, she said, "If I do not...?"

Merlin had apparently expected her to ask. He answered immediately. "Then there is only one person in this earth who can, and will, oppose you."

"I have a dagger," Petra said idly, holding the blade up in front of her eyes, watching the gloomy evening light play along its sooty length.

Merlin nodded slowly, gravely. "Indeed you do," he replied. "And only you can choose how and if you will ever use it."

Petra nodded, watching the light slide along the edge of the blade. It was somehow both comforting and maddening. Finally, she lowered the dagger and looked across the room.

Merlin's chair was empty. Petra was not particularly surprised.

# *Four*

P etra's last full day in the Morganstern household dawned cold but sunny. The corners of the windows were frozen with dew, now beading and dripping as the sun warmed the air. Petra arose feeling better than she had in months. She took her work dress out of the closet, and then paused, looking at it in her hand. It was drab, made of a dull brown calico with plain black buttons. She shook her head at it, and then hung it up again. Hangers rattled as she pushed the contents of the closet aside, reaching for something in the back. When she withdrew, she was holding a pale yellow dress with mother-of-pearl buttons. It was her Sunday dress, although it had been years—since grandmother had died, in fact—since the Morgansterns had attended a church. Petra smiled at it slightly, and then carried it to her window, moving into the light of the morning sunbeam. With thoughtless, teenage grace, she changed out of her nightdress and slipped into the pale yellow dress. It felt cool and good as it draped over her. Petra turned to look at herself in the cracked cheval mirror. Golden sunbeams painted her right side, making the dress virtually glow. It was a rather old dress, and hardly stylish, but it transformed her. She was pretty. Petra smiled at herself in the mirror and sighed.

She was hardly aware of it, but Petra had made a decision. She had lived so long in uncertainty that she'd forgotten the simple happiness of arriving at a conclusion and not looking back. She nodded to herself in the mirror, and then turned resolutely. She gripped the ratty curtains over her single window and stripped them open, letting the sunlight pour into the room. Through the window, Petra could see the side yard, the garden, the stretch of woods between the house and the lake. Mist rose beyond the trees like a white wraith, burning away in the golden morning light. Dew sparkled in the grass and frosted the trees. It was strangely beautiful, in spite of everything. Petra wondered if she'd ever seen the farm this way before, at least since she'd been very young—seen it for the simple, beautiful thing it was. The woods and the fields, the garden and the lake, even the Wishing Tree with its weight of fieldstones around its rooted feet, none of it was tainted by the ugliness that lived in the house. The house was Phyllis' domain, and it belonged to her, but not the rest. The rest of the farm belonged to Petra and Grandfather Warren and the memory of Petra's grandmother. It belonged to the ghost of Petra's own mother, who had grown up here in happier times. The farm was good. Petra would miss it.

She came down the stairs slowly, thoughtfully, and Izzy was already there, seated at the table, methodically eating a bowl of plain oatmeal.

"It's about time," Phyllis proclaimed sternly, glancing up at Petra from the sink, her eyes steely. Petra smiled at her and sat down at the table. Phyllis blinked, her hands buried in the sink, red and sudsy up to her elbows. "What are you dressed for, young lady? The Prince's ball? Are we fancying ourselves in a Cinderella mood today, my dear?"

Petra shook her head, pulling a bowl toward her. "It's such a lovely day. I thought it'd be nice to dress for it for once. I hope you don't object."

"It's about time," Phyllis proclaimed sternly,
glancing up at Petra from the sink, her eyes steely.

Phyllis studied Petra for a long moment, her eyes narrowed very slightly. Finally she seemed to dismiss her. "Suit yourself. You only have one nice dress. If you wish to destroy it by working in it, it's entirely on your head, although it'd probably break your poor grandfather's heart."

"I'm glad you don't object, Mother," Petra said lightly.

Phyllis glanced sharply back at her again, her eyebrows simultaneously knitted and raised. She didn't say anything, even though she seemed to want to.

Petra was enjoying herself. It was so easy to manipulate the horrible woman, once you truly understood what mattered to her. Petra sensed Phyllis' tense glance but pretended not to notice.

After a minute, Petra turned to Izzy. "Would you like to go out and scamper with me for a little while tonight, Iz?"

"She'll hardly have time for that," Phyllis interjected in a steely voice, having resumed her washing. "She leaves tomorrow morning at dawn, if you recall. She has more than enough packing and chores to keep her busy all day, and then it'll be early to bed, and that's that."

Izzy hadn't looked up from the paste of her oatmeal. She stirred it listlessly.

"That's all right," Petra answered brightly. "I don't have that much to do today. I'll help Izzy finish her chores and pack, and it'll leave us plenty of time to play for a bit after dinner, before bedtime. After all, it may be awhile before we have that chance again, right Iz?"

Phyllis actually snorted a derisive laugh. "That's for sure," she muttered.

Petra glanced at the back of the woman's head, narrowing her eyes. "Of course, there will be your visits home," she said, talking to Izzy but still watching Phyllis. "We'll have time to play then, too. Won't that be fun?"

Now it seemed to be Phyllis' turn to enjoy herself. "Oh, I wouldn't be too sure about that," she answered, noisily stacking plates in the dish drainer. "One can never be too sure about the future. Situations can change in a moments' notice. Just ask 'Papa Warren' about that."

Petra frowned tightly, studying the horrible woman's scrawny neck, the merciless bun of her greying hair. Could Phyllis actually be referring to the death of Petra's grandmother? Even she wouldn't say something so callous and mean, would she? Or was she referring to something else? It occurred to Petra that perhaps she wasn't the only one planning something. Phyllis was still stewing with two different kinds of rage, and Petra had known that she was merely biding her time, working out the best plan for having her petty revenge. But what could the horrible woman be up to? What, really, was she capable of?

Petra decided it couldn't possibly matter. Not to her. If Phyllis was planning something, Grandfather Warren would surely know about it. After all, whether he liked it or not, he could read her thoughts and intentions. That skill was the last vestige of his wizarding blood, and he could no sooner turn it off than he could stop breathing. He was not a strong man, but he would never allow Phyllis to hurt Petra. He would die first.

Thinking that, Petra finished her meager breakfast and embarked on her day of chores and helping Izzy.

It was not a bad day. As Petra had long ago learned, manual labor has its own special pleasantness. Unlike school work and studying, physical work allows the mind to wander free, strung out on the cord of boredom to explore its own fancies and waking dreams. Growing up on a farm, Petra had, in fact, lived much of her life in that trancelike world of imagination, daydreaming away while her body toiled at some repetitive, purely physical task. Petra had come to love the feeling of falling into bed each night utterly exhausted. In fact, the beginning of all of her previous school terms had been plagued by short bouts of insomnia, her body unused to the inverted world of mental work and sedentary living. Farm life was never particularly exciting, and it was quite often physically demanding, but it was not a bad life. Petra thought these things as she moved throughout her last day on the farm, working, more often than not, alongside Izzy.

In Petra's presence, Izzy barely seemed slow at all. Tasks that Izzy could barely manage under Phyllis' impatient instruction, she performed with Petra swiftly and gracefully. Petra had always believed she was simply a better teacher than Phyllis, mainly because she was more patient and gentle with the girl. But now Petra wondered. Merlin had said that a sorceress drew her power from the world around her; what if it was also possible for a sorceress to feed power into her environment? It made sense, really. Perhaps, in Petra's presence, Izzy really did teeter on the edge of witch-hood, as the girl had so often wished. Petra hesitated to consider it—it was such a happy thought that it was a little heartbreaking. And yet, Petra remembered the stories about Merlin himself, about how he had taught magic to the entirely human and nonmagical 'Lady of the

Lake', Judith, who was to have been his wife. Normal witches and wizards could no sooner teach magic to average humans than they could teach a mosquito to speak French. But perhaps sorcerers and sorceresses could impart a shadow of their power, that part of their power that comes from nature all around, to even a mentally challenged human. Petra thought on this as she and Izzy toiled. She wondered what Phyllis would say if she could see her daughter working the way she did in Petra's presence. Would it change her mind about her? Sadly, Petra thought it wouldn't. Phyllis would merely accuse Petra of puppeting the girl, influencing her with her unnatural, witchy arts.

And in all honesty, Petra did not know that Phyllis wouldn't be right.

By the time evening began to descend on the farm and dinner was over, Petra and Izzy had, in fact, succeeded in getting Izzy's meager closet and toiletries packed into the small secondhand trunk. Their duties were finished, even after Phyllis' addition of several more chores late in the afternoon. Despite this, Phyllis was unwilling to allow the two girls to go out and "scamper", as Petra had promised Izzy.

"I'll not have you taking her out into the fields and filling her head with your inane thoughts and foolishness," Phyllis finally said, not looking up from her business. "I've worked for years to keep you from ruining her silly, addled brain with your unnatural freakishness. I know you think this is your last chance at her, but I won't have it." Strangely, Phyllis seemed even more distracted than usual. She moved around the house in a harried, preoccupied way. Grandfather Warren had once again retired to the barn for the night, leaving Petra to fend for herself with the horrid woman. Petra followed her from room to room.

"I honestly don't know what you're talking about," she said, affecting an air of vapid innocence. "I just want to enjoy one last day with the girl I grew up with before she goes away. Surely you won't deny—"

"I will and I am," Phyllis retorted sharply, glancing up and turning to Petra. "You can pretend all you want with me, you little witch, but I know better. I can see right through you. You had your chance to interfere, and it didn't work. Do you understand? You probably thought you'd won that day in the parlor with Percival, but you were greatly mistaken. I know what's best for Izabella, regardless of what you or your Grandfather think."

Petra was surprised to realize that she didn't feel the slightest bit piqued by Phyllis' words. Phyllis was indeed afraid of her, and out of that fear she was playing her best hand, struggling to keep her iron-grip on the household for just one more, all-important day. As far as Phyllis was concerned, tomorrow wasn't important; if she could only maintain control until then, it wouldn't matter anymore. It would be too late for Petra to do anything.

"I can't imagine what you're talking about, Mother," Petra said, shaking her head sadly.

"DON'T CALL ME THAT!" Phyllis nearly shrieked, her voice cracking. Nearby, Izzy jumped, dropping the sock she'd been darning. She looked up, frightened. Phyllis lowered her voice, but her eyes were alive with rage; they very nearly sparked. "*Don't* you have the gall," she rasped. "Calling *me* your mother. Your mother is *dead*. Do you hear me? And she should count herself lucky! She didn't have to watch you grow up into the pathetic, aimless, troublemaker that you are! Now, get out of my sight before I get angry, you little *witch*!"

Petra simply stared at the raging, trembling woman. Livid red rode high in Phyllis' cheeks and her eyes seemed to be vibrating in their sockets.

Petra drew a long breath. In a lilting, sing-song voice, she said, "I am not a witch,"

Phyllis mistook the tone of Petra's voice for repentance. She drew herself to her full height. "That's the most sensible thing you've said in years," she replied, exhaling a pent-up breath. "Enough of this. Izzy, to bed with you. I will awake you at dawn, and I want you ready to go immediately. *You*, on the other hand," she said, raising an eyebrow at Petra, "I don't care *what* you do with yourself. As long as you stay out of my way."

And she turned and stalked off, leaving the two girls alone in cold silence.

Night descended fully as Petra sat in her room, staring out of the window. She hadn't moved in hours, ever since she'd entered the room and placed the narrow chair in the middle of the floor. She still wore her yellow dress, and despite Phyllis' warnings, it was none the worse for her day of hard work. On Petra's lap was the polished black box, its lid closed.

The moon had risen while she watched. It had climbed the sky, rising from beyond the woods, first yellow, and now bone white. It hung in the sky like a silver sickle, casting its light over the farm below.

Petra looked down at the box. It was comforting, having come to a decision. Soon, she would know exactly what she had to do. It was so simple, and yet, of course, it wouldn't be easy. Petra knew she could do it this time. After all, it really was best for everyone. She had thought that before, too, but she hadn't really known it. *Knowing* it made all the difference in the world.

Several minutes went by, and the house remained perfectly still all around her.

Finally, Petra stood. She placed the black box on the dresser. In the mirror, her own face looked back at her. By the pale blue glow of the moon, she looked different than she had that morning. Then, in the golden glow of the sun, she'd looked pretty. Now, she looked pale, like an alabaster statue. To her own eyes, she looked cold, severe; no longer pretty, yet beautiful, like a black rose.

*I have a dagger…*

She turned away from her reflection and opened the box. The dagger laid inside, its jewels sparkling and its sooty blade winking moonlight. Carefully, almost reverently, Petra took it by the handle. She shivered.

A moment later, she had left the room. In her wake, the door swung slightly on its old hinges, not producing the slightest creak.

On the bed, lying in the center of a shaft of pale moonlight, was a dark shape, long and thin, like a slash of ink. It was Petra's wand.

It had a crack running along its entire length, splitting it neatly in half.

There was only one window in the upstairs hall. It stood at the end, overlooking the first floor landing, and was covered with a set of long velvet curtains so that only the faintest sliver of night sky was visible. Petra moved along the dark hallway, long accustomed to navigating its length with no light. She moved silently past the round-framed portraits of her great grandparents, stepping thoughtlessly around the rickety credenza that stood opposite the bathroom door. Her bare feet made no noise on the threadbare runner.

She stopped. The door to Phyllis' and Grandfather's room was closed firmly, as always. Petra stood in the impenetrable darkness outside the door and listened. After a minute, she fancied she could hear the slow, subtle tide of deep breathing coming from behind the thick oak. Phyllis was inside, the coals of her rage banked and dulled, but not extinct, even in sleep. Her dreams were like fields of thorns, snagged and tangled. Petra could see them in her mind's eye, but she only looked fleetingly, assuring herself that the older woman was indeed buried deep within them. In the hall, Petra looked down at the old, tarnished doorknob. She touched it very lightly with her left hand.

*Sleep,* she said with her thoughts. *Sleep long. Sleep well. Hear nothing.*

She waited another minute, fingering the dagger in her right hand. Satisfied, she crept away from the door, approaching the last door on the opposite side of the hall.

Izzy's door.

"I've never been out this late before," Izzy whispered giddily, running out into the dewy grass of the garden. The air was still and cool around them, full of the solemnity of night. Crickets sang their ringing chorus in the woods. A scatter of moon-frosted clouds sailed high overhead like sentinels. Petra smiled as the younger girl pranced barefoot through the high grass, raising her nimble ankles like a gazelle. She held her arms out on either side and threw her head back to the sickle moon. "I didn't think I'd be able to stay awake, like you said, but I talked to my dolls and they kept me company. It was easy! It felt like no time had passed at all!"

Petra kept her voice low, even though she knew it wasn't really necessary. "This is fun, isn't it, Iz? I used to do this a lot when I was little."

"It *is* fun," Izzy agreed, circling back to Petra and grabbing her hand, lacing their fingers together. "But it's a bit wild, too, and a bit scary. Like Halloween night, but real. Right? This is what witches do all the time, don't they?"

*Petra smiled as the younger girl pranced barefoot through the high grass.*

Petra nodded, indulging the girl. "They do. They dance in the woods at midnight, with big bonfires and silver swords. Sometimes the stars fly down and join them, and the owls sing along. It's quite a party."

Izzy looked up at Petra as they walked, her eyes sober. "Do they really? Are you teasing me?"

Petra laughed. "I'd never tease you, Iz. I might stretch the truth a wee bit every now and then, but if it isn't true, it should be. Why do you ask?"

Izzy sighed in a businesslike manner, looking down at her bare feet as she walked alongside Petra. "Well, it's only that Papa Warren says that the stars are just big, giant balls of burning stuff, not magical princes and princesses and things, like in the stories."

Petra shrugged. "Both things can be true, you know. Maybe the stars really are big balls of burning gas *and* shining noble people, all at the same time."

Izzy frowned and shook her head. "That doesn't make any sense."

"Sure it does," Petra replied, warming to the topic. "Look at the trees there in the woods. What you *see* is just a bunch of wood and branches and leaves growing out of the ground, right? What you *don't* see are the spirits of the trees, the naiads and dryads."

The girl glanced up at the dark mass of trees ahead, creaking softly in the high night breezes. "The trees have spirits?"

"Sure they do. I've never seen one, but I know someone who can talk to them. They're beautiful and very solemn. They move very, very slowly, because to a tree, human time is like ant time to us. They measure their days in years, not hours."

Izzy didn't seem convinced. "How come we can't see them?"

Petra looked up as they entered the edge of the woods. "I don't know. Maybe they live in a part of the world that we can't see. Maybe *we* live in a part of the world *they* can't see. Maybe we only see their woodsy bodies and they only see some different part of us, some part of us we don't even know about."

"Our wake," Izzy said suddenly, her eyes widening.

Petra glanced down at her, confused. "Our what?"

"Our wake!" the girl repeated with almost comical impatience. "Like the men on the boats down in the fishing village. Papa Warren says the fish can't see the boats, but they can feel the wake that the boat makes. Maybe we only see the trees' woodsy bodies and the trees only sense our wakes when we go by!"

Petra had a strange feeling that Izzy was more right than even she knew. It wasn't just that her answer made sense. It was that it somehow seemed to be echoed by the trees themselves, as if somehow, silently, they were murmuring assent. Again, fleetingly, Petra thought of the idea that she'd had earlier in the day, when she and Izzy had been working together, about how Izzy seemed to tremble on the very edge of actual witch-hood when she was in Petra's presence. It was as if something inside Petra plugged into something inside Izzy, lighting her up, powering some special part of the girl that fate had cruelly neglected to wire.

Leaves crunched under their feet as they moved through the trees. After a minute, Izzy said, "So what should we do?"

Petra looked up. "I'm going to show you something."

"Oh! What is it?"

Petra stopped and took a deep breath. "This," she said, indicating the hollow before them.

Izzy didn't say anything at first. She walked into the clearing, circling around the old stone cairns, her brow slightly furrowed. Finally, stopping, she said, "What are they?"

Petra walked around the clearing to stand next to the younger girl. "I used to think they were the graves of my parents, but now... I think they're us."

Izzy grimaced thoughtfully. "You made them?"

"I did. A long time ago."

Several more seconds passed. Izzy looked up at Petra, one corner of her mouth cinched up critically. "I'd have thought they'd be prettier than that if they were us."

Petra couldn't help laughing happily. "Have a seat, Iz. Right here next to me on this log."

The two girls settled onto the old fallen tree, smoothing their dresses over their knees. Petra put her left arm around her sister and looked toward the cairns. In the deep blue moonlight, the hollow once again looked like a magical, underwater panorama, full of subtle motion and invisible depths. A subtle breeze pushed through the clearing, lifting the dead leaves and carrying them between the cairns, singing a low note in the treetops. And quietly, almost imperceptibly, the vines that entwined the cairns began to move. They shifted and rustled, producing first a soft hiss, and then a crackle. Izzy drew a long gasp, her eyes widening. Petra concentrated. Finally, both cairns produced a series of soft pops, and flowers bloomed from the vines, completely covering both shapes. The one on the left bore pale golden flowers, while the larger one on the right was covered in black roses, their petals almost purple in the moonlight. The flowers bobbed and nodded in the breeze, spreading their mingled perfume through the hollow.

"Wow!" Izzy breathed, and spontaneously clapped her hands in delight. "How'd that happen? Was it the dryads? Or did *you* do it?"

"I think we did it together," Petra said, smiling.

"I'm the one with the yellow flowers, like my hair," Izzy said, pointing. "You're the one with the black roses, because your hair is dark."

Petra nodded again, still smiling. She hadn't intended to make the flowers bloom different colors. Growing up, when these cairns had been monuments to her dead parents, they had always bloomed red, without exception.

"That was cool," Izzy said, snuggling against Petra and sighing deeply. "Especially because it's night. It's just like we're real witches. I mean, both of us, right? But no dancing stars or singing owls. No silver swords."

"At least not yet," Petra replied.

After a minute, Izzy grew restless. "I can't sit still for long," she said, climbing to her feet and looking around the hollow. "It makes me sleepy. I bet I could sleep right here, on a pile of leaves. That would be nice, wouldn't it? With just the moon looking down on us, and no one else. That would be lovely, I think."

Petra stood as well, brushing bits of bark from her bottom. "It would be very lovely."

"Are we going back now?" Izzy asked, looking up at the taller girl.

Petra shook her head slightly, still looking at the cairns and their nodding, fragrant flowers. "Not yet. I have one more thing to show you."

Izzy took Petra's right hand again and they walked on, climbing the leaf strewn slope of the hollow. Neither spoke until they reached the edge of the trees, where the sky opened up before them once again.

Izzy suddenly stopped walking, pulling Petra's arm taut until she also stopped.

"What?" Petra asked, looking back at the girl's wide eyes.

"I don't want to go there," Izzy said flatly, her eyes not moving from the view in front of her.

"What? Why not? It's just the lake. You've been down there with me a hundred times."

Izzy shook her head. Dimly, Petra could hear the *lap-lap* of the waves on the rocky shore. The sound soothed her, called to her. It seemed to be having quite the opposite effect on Izzy. "I just don't want to go down there, that's all."

"It'll be all right, Iz," Petra said soothingly. "I'll hold your hand the whole time. I know it's a little scary, but that's what makes it fun, right? Just like Halloween."

Izzy finally looked up at Petra, her eyes big and serious. She studied Petra's face, and then glanced back to the lake, to the long, shimmering band of moonlight reflected on its surface. Finally, she nodded her head, once, cautiously.

Together the two girls walked down the path toward the dock. Apart from the gentle lapping of the waves, the night was remarkably quiet. Petra realized that even the crickets had ceased their constant song. The moon looked down like a monstrous, squinting eye.

Izzy stopped again on the top step of the dock, her face grave and pale. "I don't want to go any further, Petra."

Petra still held her sister's hand. For a moment, the smell of a rotting fish spiked in her nostrils, repelling her, but then the breeze carried it away. They were nearly there. Everything was going to be all right. "Just a little teensy bit further, Iz," Petra said, smiling. "I want to show you one more thing, but I need your help."

The girl didn't budge. "What is it?" she asked, her eyes sharp, watchful.

Petra's smile broadened slightly and her eyes twinkled. "It's a secret," she whispered.

Izzy's grip on Petra's left hand loosened. It was a small thing, almost impossible to notice, but Petra noticed it nonetheless. Izzy looked out at the lake again. "I don't like secrets."

"You'll like this one," Petra soothed. "Just a little bit further. For me."

Finally, the younger girl relaxed slightly. She carefully stepped down the stairs onto the wooden planks of the dock, following Petra. Together, they walked into the cool smell of the water, moving slowly out over the gently lapping waves. Izzy lagged half a step behind Petra. Gently, Petra tightened her grip on the younger girl's hand.

"What is it you want to show me," Izzy said in a small voice. "This is far enough. I want to stop."

"Only two more steps," Petra replied, her own voice barely above a whisper. "Right here, at the edge."

"You already showed me this," Izzy suddenly said, her voice rising a little. "The gazebo at the bottom of the lake. It was creepy then, in the sunset light. I don't want to see it now. It won't be fun at night. Please, Petra."

"That's not what I want to show you," Petra said, distracted, drawing her sister forward.

"Then what, Petra? What are we here to see?"

Petra finally turned to Izzy, her eyes shining. They were dark and eerily flat. There were tears standing in them. "My mother," she replied in a strangely dead voice.

Petra was still holding Izzy's right hand in her left. She pulled the girl's hand upwards, simultaneously raising her own right hand. In it, the dagger glinted horribly, moonlight shifting along the dark blade.

"No!" Izzy squealed, pulling away. Petra's grip on the younger girl's wrist was like a vice.

"Stop fighting, Iz," Petra said, struggling to hold the girl's hand steady. "It'll only hurt for a moment."

Izzy pulled as hard as she could, and then rammed the heel of her free hand onto Petra's fist for leverage. The two girls struggled in the darkness. "What are you doing?" Izzy gasped, her voice a high whine. "Petra, stop!"

"Just a little blood, Iz," Petra replied evenly. "That's all I need. Nothing else will do. I don't need to bring her all the way back; just enough to be able to talk to her. I need my mum. She'll tell me what to do, Iz. She'll tell us both. It'll be fine, just stop *fighting*…!"

Izzy was crying as she struggled, becoming desperate. All she knew was that the bigger girl had a knife and was planning to hurt her with it. She kicked and strained, turning away from the end of the dock. Petra yanked her back, baring her teeth in the moonlight. Her face looked horrible, almost deathly. "Just a single cut on your palm. That's all. A few drops of your blood and it'll all be over. Ugh! *Stop fighting.* I don't want to *hurt* you, Iz… don't make me—"

Izzy shrieked and lunged as hard as she could, utterly panicked. Her foot slipped on the dewy surface on the dock and she dipped, falling away. Petra lost her own balance and scrambled for a handhold, grabbing for one of the dock's pilings. There was a cry, suddenly cut off, drowned by the noise of a heavy splash. Izzy had fallen into the lake.

Petra dropped to her knees, looking for the younger girl, her eyes wild. A gurgle and another splash revealed her; she was several feet away, out of Petra's reach. She flailed, her eyes bright and horrible, her mouth full of water.

"Izzy!" Petra called, her heart suddenly leaping up into her throat. "Swim to me!"

*No!* the voice in the back room of Petra's mind said, firmly and decisively. *No… wait…*

Petra froze in place as an eerie coldness descended over her. As she looked, the girl in the water seemed to change. It wasn't Izzy at all. It was another young girl with blonde hair, a girl by the name of Lily. It was just like in her dreams, the frustrating, haunting dreams of that ultimate moment in the chamber of the pool. The girl was drowning, just as the bargain had demanded. But now, this time, the dream was real. Now, Petra really could affect the outcome.

Slowly, Petra rose to her feet, watching the pathetic splashing of the girl in the water.

She hadn't meant to kill Izzy. She'd only intended to use her blood, just enough to talk to her mother. She hadn't planned to bring her mother back fully, even if that were possible.

*Is that really true?* The voice in the back room of her mind said, calmly, coldly. *I think not. I think this was your intent all along. I think this is why you came home in the first place. Everything has led to this. You only thought you had altered the plan when you chose to save the girl Lily, but you hadn't changed anything. You'd only postponed the inevitable. The girl must die. Only then will you have peace.*

And after all, what did Izzy have to live for? Was she not better off this way as well? Better to die here, on the edge of her last night of youth and innocence, than sixty years later, used up, spent, herded along through life like an animal.

*No one will know,* the voice soothed. *Her body will eventually be found, but they will believe she died at her own hand, deliberately or as an accident. You will mourn her properly. You will erect a monument to her memory, which is more than her own mother would do. You will make it right. You, with your own mother at your side.*

It was actually happening. Izzy dipped beneath the surface once more. Her hands flailed weakly, pathetically, fluttering over the rippling waves.

Petra turned. She looked back along the length of the dock, and then cast her eyes around the perimeter of the lake. Her brow furrowed slightly.

"No one is coming," she said to herself, wonderingly.

*No, the boy James does not come this time,* the voice concurred, exultantly. *No Merlinus. No one. The misguided force of good has no voice here. 'Good' is a myth. There is only balance. There is only power. Nothing else matters.*

The voice was right. No one was coming. No one was going to stop her. She was going to succeed.

Petra looked out over the water again. Izzy's small hands no longer flailed at the surface. The girl was nowhere to be seen, but surely she was not dead yet. How long could a body live without air? Petra tried to dip her mind into the dark waters, but they were strangely impenetrable; she could sense nothing at all. Why should it matter, anyway? Tears welled in Petra's eyes.

In the center of the lake, a figure was rising. Petra recognized the shape by now. Her mother looked at her across the water. Petra drew a hitching breath. Slowly, she shook her head.

Her wand was gone. Broken. She could no longer remember how to do the magic without it.

She tried anyway.

*What are you doing,* the voice in the back room of her mind asked warily.

"You are right," Petra said calmly, raising her arms out over the water. "No one is coming. No one is going to interfere with my choice."

The voice seemed to be growing alarmed. *Then what are you* doing? It demanded sternly.

"*I* am being the voice of good," Petra replied firmly, quietly. "I am choosing it myself. No one is making me. I am choosing to do right, despite everything I have longed for and dreamed of. And this time, it is my choice entirely."

Petra concentrated. She searched the water with her mind, willing it to reveal its secrets. It remained as dark and featureless as pitch. In the center of the lake, the figure of her mother stood atop the waves, its reflection cast across the band of shimmering moonlight. The figure began to walk slowly toward the dock.

*Don't be a fool. You believed the same thing in the chamber of the pool. You thought you had changed the course of destiny, and yet here you are now. You changed* nothing. *You only postponed the inevitable!*

Amazingly, Petra almost laughed. "You know, that's the second time I've heard that today," she said, gritting her teeth and concentrating. "And you know what else?" she went on, lowering her voice to a hoarse whisper. "I think you're *both* wrong."

Petra again sent her mind into murky black depths of the lake. It was amazingly cold, utterly featureless. The black water almost seemed to fight back against her, to thwart her. There was nothing there for her to grasp. Or was there? In her mind, she groped, trying to remember the essential shape of it, conjuring it in her deepest memories. It was still there, of course, and now that she'd invoked it in her mind, the lake could no longer hide its reality. Still, there was no way she could move it, even if she'd had her wand. It was impossible, and yet it was her only option. She reached, both with her mind and her hands, trying to reawaken those long dormant powers.

Something in the water began to move—something very large.

Across the lake, the figure of Petra's mother stopped walking toward her. Still in silhouette, the shadowy shape raised its arms, imploringly. Slowly, it began to sink again.

*You are not the only one with powers at your disposal,* the voice in the back room of Petra's mind said menacingly.

As it spoke, something shot out across the water, emanating from beneath the dock. It was like a white finger, and Petra realized it was a tendril of ice. Coldness enveloped Petra's left hand, and she realized that she herself was casting the ice spell. She tried to stop it, but she couldn't fight against it *and* hold onto the object in the water; it was too much effort.

*I am you, and you are me. You cannot choose light while I choose darkness. You can no sooner disrupt your destiny than you can tear yourself in half.*

The icy tendril crackled across the lake, creating a snaking, frozen bridge. It met the feet of the figure of Petra's mother, and amazingly, it lifted the figure back onto the surface, buoying it up. The dark figure began to walk again, stepping silently along the frozen bridge.

It wasn't working. Petra was losing the shape beneath the water. It was probably no use, anyway. Izzy *had* to be dead. It was too late. The figure of Petra's mother was only a few paces away. Petra could see the sad smile on her mother's face as she approached, her arms raised as if to embrace her.

*Give in. Good is a myth. All that matters is power. All that matters is getting back that which you've lost. Embrace your destiny or die fighting it. You are not good. There is no such thing. You know that now, don't you?*

Petra looked at the face of her mother. All she had to do was reach down and take her hand, help her up from the ice bridge and onto the dock. It would be over, finally. The voice was probably right.

And suddenly, Petra realized that she didn't care.

She narrowed her eyes. There were no tears in them now. She stared into the face of her dead mother, and her own face hardened, became terrible, almost goddesslike. "Good is only a myth if good people stop believing in it," she said. She was no longer speaking to the voice in the back room of her mind, neither was she speaking to the wraith of her mother. She was speaking only to Petra, herself. "It may be futile, but it's better to die trying than not to try. I may not be good, but neither am I evil. I'm caught right in the middle. Which direction I go is up to no one but *me*."

She didn't reach for her mother, but she reached. She closed her eyes, shutting everything else out, and concentrated on that shape in the water. And *pulled*.

The water roiled beneath the dock, as if something massive were pushing up beneath it. The ice bridge cracked, then shattered, disintegrating into the force of the swell. Unseen by Petra, the figure of her mother sank into the boiling cauldron of the lake, the face unchanging, always watching the girl on the dock. The watery wraith fell away. In its place, something else began to rise. It was a long, tapered length of wood, still crusted with bits of white paint. It grew out of the lake, rising, followed by a widening dome of rotten cedar shingles; a conical roof. Great chunks of shingles were missing, revealing the bleached wooden bones of the structure. Water thundered off the shape as it rose into the moonlight, shedding the weight of the lake's depths. Petra still did not open her eyes. Her face was almost serene now, as if she had finally realized something, as if some great weight had been taken off her heart and mind. Gently, she raised her arms, and the enormous shape heaved completely out of the water before her, pushing back a great scar of waves on the lake's surface.

The waterlogged gazebo hung in the air over its dark reflection, seaweed dripping from it in great sodden curtains. In defiance of its warped and rotted supports, the structure stood exactly where it had been built, decades earlier, right at the end of the dock. Its arched doorway loomed directly in front of Petra. She opened her eyes and looked down.

There, lying in the center of the gazebo's muddy wooden floor, looking tiny and pathetic, was Izzy.

Petra walked into the gazebo, hearing the steady patter of water that still rained from its rotten roof, and knelt by her sister. Izzy lay curled on her side, her legs tangled together, her blonde hair lying lank over her face, hiding it. Petra gently pushed the hair back from the girl's pale face.

"Izzy," she said softly. "I did it. I walked right up to the edge, but I didn't go over it. I had to try it. I had to know if I could do it. I made the right choice, Iz. You don't have to die. Please, don't be dead."

The girl didn't move.

Petra touched her sister's cold forehead. Slowly, she closed her eyes and cast her mind into the girl's body. Izzy was still warm inside, but dark. Petra despaired, and yet she refused to give up. She looked further. There, in the girl's deepest being, Petra found a tiny spark. It was guttering, but not gone.

*Come back, Iz,* Petra said to that spark. *It's over. The battle is done.*

The spark heard, but it didn't respond. Petra sensed that the girl was afraid and hopeless. Believing she had nothing left to live for, Izzy had decided not to fight.

*You don't have to go, Iz. If you come back, things can be different. You won't have to go to the work farm. We can go away, just us, and have all the adventures we always dreamed of.*

Petra still had her eyes closed. Beneath her hand, the girl's forehead was wet and cold, unmoving. In Petra's mind's eye, the flicker of Izzy's small life guttered.

*We can sleep on a bed of leaves,* Petra said to the tiny spark. *Just like you said. We can sleep under the stars, with no one watching us but the moon. Won't that be nice? We can go away, like you wished for the other day, when you looked at the Wishing Tree. We can go away, just you and me and the moon, forever and ever. But you have to come back, Iz. Come back, please…*

It wasn't working. The tiny spark of Izzy's life was like a mirage, teasing and fading. Had it really been there at all? Perhaps Petra had merely willed herself to see it, simply because she couldn't face the terrible truth of what she'd done. Izzy's forehead was so cold beneath Petra's hand. Her small body lay soaked and motionless, utterly dark to Petra's mind's eye.

*No, Iz. No. Don't be gone. I didn't mean for you to die. I need you. I can't go on alone. I need someone to come with me, to help me and be by my side. I don't have a mother or a father. I need my sister. Please, I don't want to sleep on that bed of leaves alone.*

Petra opened her eyes and looked down at her sister. Izzy's eyes were open. She looked up at Petra calmly. Petra smiled down at her, and then laughed with relief, tears finally spilling over her cheeks.

In a small, confidential tone of voice, Izzy asked, "Can Beatrice come, too?"

Fortunately, Izzy's trunk had already been packed in preparation for her journey to Percival Sunnyton's work farm. The girls crept into the house to retrieve it, carrying it between them through the darkened hall, and down the stairs. They bumped the wall once as they turned the landing, but Petra knew it wouldn't matter. Phyllis was deeply asleep, the coal of her rage barely an ember. Petra couldn't sense grandfather Warren at all. She was a little sad to leave him, but not much. They'd both known this day would come, and that it would probably be best for everyone.

Outside, Petra carried the trunk herself, leading Izzy back out to the woods. There, they rested the trunk next to the cairns, and Petra retrieved the only possession that mattered to her: her broom.

It wasn't going to be easy, but with any luck, she'd not have to manage their escape alone. Leaving Izzy seated on her trunk, Petra walked backwards up the leaf-strewn slope of the hollow, scanning the branches above.

"Caelia," she called softly.

Something moved in the trees, a dark shape against the indigo sky. A branch creaked as the figure launched from it. It circled through the trees, spiraling downward on strong wings. Izzy watched, transfixed, as the shape flapped once, twice, and landed easily on top of one of the cairns, the one that was still covered in black roses. It was an owl, huge and brown, with somber orange eyes that blinked slowly as Petra approached.

"Caelia, the time has come. You know what to do and who to go to. Here is the note. I hope you've had a good dinner of field mice tonight, because you'll need it. Fly as fast as you can, and come find us wherever we are when you're finished. All right?"

The great horned owl squawked once in a businesslike manner. Immediately, she unfurled her wings and balanced on the top of the cairn for a moment. With a gust of night air and a clap of wings, she launched. Izzy ducked as the bird's shadow flickered over her. A moment later, Caelia was gone, soaring silently out of the forest and into the dark sky.

"I didn't know you had an owl," Izzy said, yawning.

"Nobody did," Petra admitted. "Not even Grandfather. You'll get used to it, though. It's better than waiting for the postman, at any rate, and she can find us no matter where we are. She's a very smart owl."

"Who are we sending post to at this time of night?"

Petra sighed, and then shivered. It had turned into a very cold night. "Help, I hope," she replied.

The girls began to climb the slope again, leading out of the hollow, carrying Izzy's trunk between them. Petra had her broom slung over her shoulder in her right hand.

"We need to get away from the house," she said quietly. "For now, that's all that matters."

After a minute, Izzy asked, "Will we ever come back again?"

"I don't think so, Iz."

Izzy nodded thoughtfully. "Will we ever see my mother again?"

Petra looked down at the girl as they walked out of the perimeter of the trees. "I don't think so, Iz. Sorry."

Izzy's face remained impassive as she looked aside at the dark house. After a long moment, she drew a quick sigh, dismissing the house, and everyone in it. She would probably cry, eventually, over leaving her mother, despite everything, but for now, Izzy seemed ready to move on. A few steps later, she said, "Will we need to change our names?"

Petra hadn't thought about it, but it seemed like a good idea. "Sure, Iz. Would you like that?"

"I've never liked the name Izabella," the girl answered. "I want to be called Victoria. Or Penelope."

"Maybe both," Petra suggested. "Victoria Penelope. But never Vicky Penny."

Izzy grimaced in disgust. "*Never* Vicky Penny. What about you? Will you change your name?"

Petra considered it for a long moment. She nodded. "Yes, I think a name change is in order. No more Petra Morganstern. After tonight, I don't think she even exists anymore, to tell you the truth."

"So what will your new name be?"

Petra stared straight ahead as they walked. "Morgan," she said quietly, thoughtfuly. "Just Morgan."

Izzy nodded seriously, glancing up at her sister. "I like it. Morgan. It sounds... serious. Like the name of a witch queen or something."

Petra merely looked down at the younger girl, and smiled.

They crossed the path and threaded out into Grandfather Warren's field. The field was mostly bare, leaving merely muddy furrows and the occasional weed. As they climbed the hill toward the Wishing Tree, Petra could just see the edge of the lake beyond the woods. It sparkled silently in the moonlight.

"I'm tired, Petra," Izzy said as they neared the tree. "Can we rest a minute?"

The girls angled toward the tree, dropping Izzy's small trunk near the tumble of old field stones. It couldn't hurt to allow the younger girl a rest. Most likely, she'd never stayed up all night in her entire life, and Petra would need her to be alert throughout the coming day.

Petra took off her cloak and spread it on the grassy swell at the base of the tree. "Here, Iz, lie down for a bit. I'll keep watch and we'll go on in a little while. It'll be all right."

"Really?" the girl said, immediately dropping to her hands and knees on the cloak. The springy grass beneath formed a wonderfully soft mattress. "Lie down with me and keep me warm, all right? It'll be like a sleepover."

Petra joined her sister on the cloak, lying down on her back and placing the palm of her right hand under her head. Izzy snuggled next to her, curling up with her back to Petra's side. She was quite warm, and Petra was mildly surprised at how comfortable it was. She stared up through the branches of the Wishing Tree, to the strew of stars far above.

"Petra?" Izzy said, not turning.

"The name's Morgan," Petra said, smiling.

"Morgan," Izzy amended easily. "You really scared me tonight."

"I know, Iz. I'm very sorry. I… I never should have involved you. But it's over now. It's going to be all right."

A minute went by, and Petra thought the girl had fallen asleep. Then: "Will you ever scare me like that again?"

Petra thought about it for a long moment. She wanted to be as honest with Izzy as possible, especially now. "I can't promise I'll never scare you again, Iz. But I can promise that I will never scare you like *that* again. I can promise that while I might scare you, I'll never again make you fear me. I'll look out for you, no matter what. Do you understand?"

The girl seemed to consider this. After a moment, Petra sensed Izzy nod. "I'm glad. I don't think I could come with you, otherwise."

"Good. I'm glad you're coming with me," Petra said quietly. "I wouldn't have it any other way, Iz."

"The name's Victoria," Izzy muttered. Petra smiled. Finally, the girl began to drift to sleep.

Petra lay with her eyes open, watching the indigo sky through the lace of branches. It was a very still night. The grass around made only the barest whisper in the breeze.

Petra still wore her yellow Sunday dress, with only a rough woolen jumper pulled over it. That and her broom were her only possessions; she'd taken nothing else from her own room. Her wand still lay broken on her bed, and the black wooden box still sat on her dresser, empty, its lid pushed open. She'd not need them anymore.

She had lost the dagger. It had fallen from her hand when Izzy had slipped, dropped while Petra had scrambled for a handhold. Cautiously, Petra cast her mind out over the farm, focusing on the lake. She dipped into its cold depths, doubting she'd find the dagger in that expanse of dark murk. To her shock, it revealed itself immediately, as if it were a magnet, drawing her. The lake was unusually deep, shaped like a steep funnel that dipped into a natural, subterranean spring. The dagger lay on the slope of the lake's floor, deep enough that sunlight would barely reach it. Silently, from its own watery grave, it called her.

Petra closed the eye of her mind, shutting it out. She couldn't kill the voice in the back room of her mind, but she could deny it its tools. The dagger was not destroyed—perhaps it *couldn't* be—but it was lost, out of reach, its power denied. That was good enough for now.

A cloud drifted silently over the sickle moon, high above, dimming its silvery light. Petra watched it. She wouldn't sleep; she didn't even feel sleepy. But she would close her eyes, just for a few minutes. Izzy needed to rest, and Petra would let her. Just for a little while, and then they'd go. There was no harm in that. Just for a little while.

In the woods, down in the hollow, the flowers on the cairns slowly closed. The blooms vanished, and the vines relaxed. Slowly, they loosened their grip on the stone cairns. In the darkness, unseen and unheard, one of the stones fell away. It thumped to the ground and rolled to a stop. No mortal eye could have seen the difference, but the difference was there, nonetheless:

The magic had left the hollow.

# *Five*

Voices roused Petra, pulling her out of sleep, and she came only reluctantly, fighting against the nagging sounds. She was sore, cold, and wet with dew. She rolled over and found herself face down in a mass of stringy wetness. Jerking herself awake, she pushed up onto her elbows, spitting.

She was outside, lying in tall grass. Mist rose from the ground all around her, diffusing the early sunlight into a pall of grey. She seemed to be lying in an island of grass and field stones, surrounded by fog. She turned and squinted down, her eyes thick with sleep. Izzy lay next to her, wrapped in Petra's cloak. The rise and fall of her chest showed that she was still buried deep in sleep.

Petra cursed to herself, suddenly remembering everything. She herself had fallen asleep, in spite of everything. It was past dawn, and they hadn't even left the Morganstern property. She climbed shakily to her feet, steadying herself on the wet bark of the Wishing Tree.

They had to hurry, but where should they go? Carrying Izzy's trunk with them was going to slow them down considerably. Perhaps they should abandon it and resort to the broom. Izzy could ride pillion behind Petra and they could follow the steam, as Petra had done so many times in the previous years. Apart from the very occasional kid with a fishing pole, the steep, high banks of the stream formed the perfect secret highway for a broom-born witch.

Petra wandered away from the tree, trying to get her bearings. She wondered if Caelia had gotten to her destinations by now. She wondered if her message had been received and understood. She wondered what the two girls would do with themselves in the weeks and months to come. Where would they go? How long would they need to hide? So many questions. And yet, somehow, Petra wasn't afraid. She was, if anything, exhilarated. She had gone down to the lake the night before in search of answers. And to her great surprise, she had found them.

Voices. They had awoken her minutes earlier. She realized she was hearing them again, and they were growing louder. Petra's eyes widened and she turned around, looking back toward the Wishing Tree. The mist was burning away in the persistent morning sunlight, revealing the rest of the farm. There was a sudden shout and the tweet of a whistle, piercing the air.

Petra ran.

As she reached the top of the hill and bolted around the dark shape of the Wishing Tree, she saw Izzy. The girl was awake, standing several yards away, Petra's cloak still clutched around her shoulders. Her back was to Petra as she stared down the hill, toward the house.

Percival Sunnyton's truck was parked in the drive, as were two other vehicles. With a jolt of raw fear, Petra recognized they were police cars. Figures were milling in the garden, beginning to look up toward the Wishing Tree. One of the policemen was trotting up the path, his whistle still protruding from between his teeth.

Izzy turned, her eyes wide and frightened. "What do we do, Petra? Morgan? They're coming to take me with them. I'll have to go away!"

"You won't have to go with them, Iz—Victoria," Petra replied evenly, striding forward to get between the girl and the approaching figures. "Just stay behind me. I'll talk to them. It'll be all right. Do you believe me?"

"I believe you," the girl said quickly, peeking between Petra's arm and side.

"There!" a distant, shrill voice suddenly cried. Petra looked toward the sound and saw Phyllis standing on the porch, pointing. Even from her vantage point, Petra could see the look of exultant triumph on the woman's pinched face. Her eyes flashed, meeting Petra's. "That's them! Quickly! I knew it!"

Percival Sunnyton emerged from the screen door, looking from Phyllis to the Wishing Tree, spotting the two girls. Together, he and Phyllis descended the steps and hurried across the garden.

"There's no need to meet us here," Petra called, her voice ringing in the still morning air. "We're not coming back with you, and we hate long goodbyes."

The policeman with the whistle was closest, huffing as he climbed the slope of the field. He was older, quite stout, his face red and blotchy. "Why don't you just come along back to the house, miss, and we'll talk this over nice and civil-like. What do you say?"

"I say you may as well stop right there, officer, and save yourself some effort," Petra replied, raising her chin. "We're not going to be coming back, and that's that."

"Petra Morganstern, yes?" the officer panted. "And that little waif behind you is Miss Izabella Morganstern, I assume. I'm afraid things aren't quite as simple as that. We've got a warrant for your arrest, you see. Just issued this morning, thanks to that charming lady and her friend. Come along quietly, and I'm certain we can work out this little misunderstanding straight away."

Izzy cringed against Petra from behind as the policemen neared.

Suddenly, the policeman with the whistle tripped. He stumbled and fell headlong onto the muddy furrows, still several yards away.

"I'd be careful, Officer Patrick," Petra said coolly. "It can get rather treacherous out here if you don't know the lay of the land."

The policeman had dropped his whistle when he fell. He struggled to his feet, brushing himself off, scanning the ground for the whistle and swearing to himself. Suddenly, he looked up, his brow furrowed. "And just how'd you know my name, Miss?"

Behind him, the other two policemen were catching up, sauntering a bit more slowly. Sunnyton and Phyllis were following closely. Sunnyton was helping Phyllis awkwardly, offering her his elbow as they traversed the furrows.

"I knew you'd try something like this," Phyllis called out shrilly. "I was prepared, I was. It takes a lot more than a little sneak like you to pull one over on me, young lady!" To the policemen, she cried, "What are you waiting for? She's kidnapped my daughter! Get her and bring her back! I pay your salaries, so do as I say!"

Officer Patrick had regained his footing. He approached Petra a bit more slowly. "You heard the lady, my dear. Now we can do this the easy way—"

There was a wet squelch as Officer Patrick went down again, falling full-length into the muddy field. He swore loudly as his cap tumbled away, flopping into a brown puddle.

"Go back home, Phyllis," Petra called calmly. "This is a mistake. You don't want us around anyway. Go home to Grandfather Warren."

"Hah!" Phyllis barked. "As if *he'd* be any help! The two of you are thick as thieves! I'm surprised he isn't out here helping you! But I'll show him! I'll show *both* of you!"

Suddenly, Petra saw something she hadn't noticed before, something she'd been too preoccupied to recognize. She remembered the conversation in the house yesterday, remembered the way Phyllis had referred to the owner of the work farm; not as 'Mr. Sunnyton', but as 'Percival'. Even now, there he was, supporting her with his elbow, his pudgy face grim with satisfaction. Phyllis had indeed been planning something, as Petra had suspected. She'd been planning to get back at both Petra and Warren, and using the same means.

Phyllis was close enough now to see the realization dawning on Petra's face.

"You've figured out what's really going on, I see," she crowed. "It's true. Percival isn't just here for Izabella. *I'm* going with him as well, leaving this God-forsaken swamp once and for all. Frankly, I have *you* to thank for it, my dear. I'd never have realized how truly weak Warren was until he failed to stand up to you that day in the parlor. Percival is different, though, as you can see. He sees things my way entirely. I think we'll be very happy together. All *three* of us."

"No," Izzy breathed, still hiding behind Petra. "No!"

Phyllis and the policemen were nearly upon them. Phyllis was grinning, her color high with triumph. "Quiet, Izabella. Come along this moment and I won't punish you for your disobedience. Let's not keep Percival waiting."

"No!" Izzy cried again, clutching Petra.

"Look here, young lady," another of the policemen said, striding forward to meet the girls. Officer Patrick, covered in mud, was right behind him. Petra's eyes had not moved from Phyllis. Her expression was calm, her eyes narrowed.

"What the—!" the third policeman suddenly cried, dropping to one knee and reaching for his baton. A shadow flickered over him. Everyone except Petra looked up, eyes wide, stunned.

The air seemed full of inexplicable figures, swooping in from all directions. The shapes swirled down over the field, cloaks snapping behind them.

"What's all this!" Officer Patrick cried, reaching for his truncheon. A red flash struck him as he pulled his weapon, and the unfortunate policeman tumbled to the muddy field for the third time, unconscious.

"Nobody else move!" a new voice called. "You aren't seeing what you think you're seeing, believe me. What you *are* seeing is impossible, of course, so feel free to faint from the sheer absurdity of it. It'll save us all a load of effort, thanks."

"Shut *up*, Damien!" a girl's voice hushed as she dropped gently from the sky on her broom. "Don't make this any worse! We'll probably end up in shackles as it is!"

"Calm down, Sabrina," another voice said coolly. "Let's just get this over with."

Three figures, two teenage boys and a girl, all on broomsticks, settled to the ground between the girls and their pursuers. The policemen backed away, their hands on their truncheons. The girl named Sabrina had thick red hair pulled back into a ponytail. Damien was short and stout, with black-framed glasses. Both had wands in their hands, pointing at the gathering on the hillside. The second boy moved behind Petra. Gently, he took Izzy's hand, leading her to the side, toward her trunk and Petra's broom.

"What are you doing?" Phyllis cried incredulously, addressing the policemen. "*Arrest* them! Arrest them all! They are accessories to a crime! Are you all blind?"

"I ain't too blind to see we're now officially outnumbered," one of the officers muttered, backing away. "Now that one of those flying kids just tazered Patrick,"

"He's not dead, you idiots! Just knocked out! For heaven's sake, they're just kids! Kids with sticks! *Arrest* them!"

Next to Phyllis, Sunnyton watched a fourth shadow circle down, swooping toward him. Caelia, the great horned owl, landed in the field right in front of him, her huge wings outstretched menacingly. He boggled at her, his lips quivering. The bird hopped toward him and squawked piercingly. Sunnyton jumped, pulling Phyllis backwards. She turned on him, her eyes wild, and angrily yanked her arm away from him.

At the top of the hill, in the shadow of the Wishing Tree, Petra spoke. "How dare you," she breathed her voice low but heard by all. She had not budged in the last minute, had never taken her eyes away from the scrawny woman with whom she had shared a house for the past decade. She took a step forward, her hands curling slowly into fists. "You awful wreck of a woman. How *dare* you!"

Phyllis glanced back at her, surprised by the outburst. "How dare I? What are you talking about?"

"How dare you share a bed with my grandfather, all the while knowing that you were leaving him for this pathetic *wretch*!"

Sunnyton blinked as if slapped. He continued to back away, looking from Petra to Phyllis. Phyllis drew herself to her full height. "Share a bed? You're more of a fool than I thought. Your grandfather has not been to bed in *days*. Not since that afternoon in the parlor. Not since I made my decision to *leave* him! Besides, what would you know of such things, you little strumpet!"

The expression of anger leaked out of Petra's face. "Not since you..." she said to herself slowly, replaying Phyllis' words. A cold, horrible realization washed over her: *grandfather would have known*. He could read Phyllis' mind—he couldn't help it, it was just part of the wizard that he was, in spite of his own denial of that magical nature. He'd have known of his wife's plan, even as she was devising it. That's why he'd stayed away... why he'd...

"Petra," the second boy said softly, moving close behind her. He had ragged black hair and piercing eyes looking out of a thin but handsome face. "We need to fly. Izzy's ready. We have to—"

A sudden pall of coldness descended over the hilltop, interrupting the boy. He shivered violently and looked around. The leaves in the

Wishing Tree crackled and grew white as the misty air froze onto them. The tall grass frosted over, spreading a white corona down the furrows of the hilltop, under the feet of those gathered. The puddle that still bore Officer Patrick's dropped hat iced over, making a sound like a Christmas bulb being crushed under a boot. The two policemen who were still conscious backed down the hill quickly, their eyes widening, their breath puffing out in white clouds. Sunnyton finally turned and bolted, loping back toward his truck, his white coat tails flapping. Sabrina and Damien looked cautiously back over their shoulders, their wands lowering distractedly in their hands.

Only Petra and Phyllis didn't move. They stared at one another over the sudden chill, their eyes locked.

"You murderess," Petra breathed.

Phyllis' eyebrows rose momentarily.

Petra took another step forward. "You never even checked on him. Did you even wonder what he was doing those nights he didn't come to bed? Did you even once go and look in on him, to see what he was doing out there in the barn?"

"He's a grown man," Phyllis muttered, "I was his wife, not his nursemaid."

"You were his murderer," Petra said with soft ferocity. "He hangs now, in the barn, dead by his own hand. He chose to end his life rather than watch you leave him. He stepped into that noose himself, but it was your hate that tied it."

"Even if what you say is true," Phyllis said, rallying. "It wasn't *my* hand that killed him. It was you. *You* turned him against me. *You* teased him about the life he'd left behind. You plagued him with regrets, made sure he was miserable in the life that he'd chosen. If it hadn't been for you, none of this would have happened. If only you could have stayed gone! But *no*, you had to return and stir things up. It's all your fault. *You're* the reason that that man chose to die as he'd lived: as a *coward!* I

*Only Petra and Phyllis didn't move.*
*They stared at one another over the sudden chill, their eyes locked.*

hope you live forever with that on your head! *You're* responsible, Petra Morganstern, not me! *Not* me!"

Petra shook her head slowly, her face hard as granite, cold as the grave. "My name..." she said softly, "Is *Morgan*."

The ground shook. Behind Petra, the Wishing Tree *moved*. It leaned to one side, creaking and crackling, as if its trunk were a monstrous snake, and suddenly, violently, the earth exploded around it. Half of the Tree's roots ripped out of the ground, taking great chunks of earth with them and knocking the piles of field stones aside. The Tree leaned in the other direction, looking like nothing so much as a giant pulling its feet out of a sandy pit. Roots tore from the earth, sending geysers of wet dirt into the air. Bits of earth pattered around Petra, but she didn't move. She stood like a statue, staring at the pale, horrified face of her nemesis. Phyllis' eyes bulged as she craned her head up, up, watching the Wishing Tree hoist itself out of its earthen bed. The ground trembled violently as the roots of the Tree slammed down, forming something like legs, something like knotted tentacles.

Petra felt someone next to her; fingers laced into hers. It was Izzy. Together, the two girls watched, calmly and apparently unafraid. The Tree stepped over them, throwing them into shadow as it blocked out the sun. Dirt pattered all around them.

Phyllis still hadn't moved. Her mouth had dropped open as her eyes bulged. The Tree's shadow fell over her, and then the massive shape twisted, leaning. Branches snaked around Phyllis, clamping her in a giant, woodsy fist. She was pulled swiftly from the ground, leaving her shoes behind.

"I knew this day would come!" she shrieked suddenly, her voice nearly lost in the creaking, moaning cacophony of the thrashing Tree. "I *knew* you'd be the death of me, you horrible girl! And I was right! I was *riiiight!*"

The Tree lumbered across the field as if in slow motion, covering it in two enormous strides. Slowly, massively, it descended toward the lake. Its final destination was obvious.

Petra watched, remembering long ago times, happier times. Back then, the gazebo had been Grandfather Warren's pride and joy. They used to have parties in there, once in every great while. The inside of the gazebo could be enchanted to be much larger than the outside. The inside could be made into a ballroom—a cathedral—if Grandfather wished. It had always been a delight to the young girl that was Petra. It was a magical place, full of wonder.

The Wishing Tree carried Phyllis, entwined in its snaking branches, down the slope to the lake. It crushed the dock underfoot as it approached the gazebo, but the gazebo remained, held up entirely by magic. It looked different in the daylight, transformed somehow. It was no longer rotted, ruined, covered in beards of seaweed. It was gloriously perfect, glowing white in the morning sunlight.

Slowly, horribly, the Wishing Tree began to enter it.

It was impossible to watch. It defied the eye. The Tree was easily three times larger than the wooden structure, and yet space seemed to become plastic where they met. The Tree squeezed through the door, cramming inside. The gazebo shuddered, but held firm, floating over its rippling reflection. The branches that imprisoned Phyllis were the last to enter. She struggled gamely, but not very convincingly. Petra almost believed the horrible woman *wanted* to go inside to her doom. She looked up at the last moment, scanning the distance for Petra. Her eyes were steely, bright and terrible. *I always knew you'd be the death of me,* they said. They were almost triumphant.

And then she was gone, pulled inside in one final, violent motion.

The gazebo shuddered, leaning, and slowly came to rest. For a long moment, it seemed to be prepared to hold fast. Then, suddenly and with perfect finality, it sank, throwing up a swell of murky green and an explosion of white water that crashed back, engulfing it. After a few seconds, all that was left was a rain of misty droplets and an expanding ripple of waves.

Izzy squeezed Petra's hand lightly. "Goodbye, Mother," she whispered.

The foursome flew above the low clouds, chasing their shadows over the billowing, sunlit shapes. Riding pillion behind Petra, Izzy clutched her sister's waist tightly, her face a circle of radiant wonder. Occasionally, as they rounded a vista of towering storm clouds or punched through a misty wall of white fog, the girl would laugh out loud. Petra marveled at the girl's shocking resilience. As she'd thought the night before, the time would surely come when Izzy—Victoria—would cry over what had happened that last morning at Morganstern farm. Like Petra, the girl that Izzy had been was surely gone, her innocence shattered when, together, they had sent the Wishing Tree after Phyllis. Blood was on their hands. Justified, perhaps, but that was a hollow comfort. These were things that would have to be dealt with later, and it wouldn't be easy. For now, however, Petra exulted in the girl's simple delight. The adventure was on, even if it had started in a horrible way. As Petra had also thought once before, perhaps life only really began once innocence died.

The dark-haired boy flew in the lead, his broom long and rather old, but well maintained. "Buckle up!" he shouted back. "We're going down, and it's going to be right nasty down there! We're just over a thunderstorm!"

"Excellent," Damien lamented sarcastically. "I just washed this thing yesterday."

"Are you two all right?" Sabrina called over to Petra and Izzy.

Petra nodded, smiling grimly into the misty wind. "Fine! Hold on tight, Victoria!"

"All right, Morgan!" the girl replied, calling over the noise of the rushing air and clutching her sister's waist. "Where are we going, anyway?"

The four brooms dipped gently, dropping into a world of wet, grey air. Thunder boomed nearby, seeming to come from the rushing clouds all around.

Morgan called back to her sister, "Did I ever tell you about my friend James?"

As afternoon wore on at Morganstern Farm, more police cars arrived. They clustered around the garden, digging muddy tracks into the grass, their lights flashing over the house and barn. Eventually, a long, black car arrived. It pulled right up to the open doors of the barn and two men produced a stretcher from the back. They didn't seem to be in any hurry.

Policemen in plain clothes stood around the hilltop in Morganstern field, puzzling over the enormous, ragged crater where a tree had supposedly been. Two of the policemen who'd initially responded to the call had claimed that the alleged tree had actually gotten up and walked away. Later, however, the two had recanted their statements, explaining that they'd been confused and, quite possibly, drugged by the horrible woman's tea. Some speculated that they had changed their stories rather quickly after the visit from the tall, bearded man in the long black cloak— the man who had claimed to be from Internal Affairs, but whose identification no one could later recall—but this was dismissed as mere conjecture and annoying conspiracy theory.

The horrible woman, one Phyllis Morganstern, formerly Phyllis Blanchefleur, had apparently fled the scene. Further investigation showed that Warren Morganstern was the *second* husband to die under suspicious circumstances while married to Ms. Blanchefleur. A warrant was issued for her arrest, ostensibly for "questioning", but there was no great effort to find the woman. She would probably turn up eventually. Probably.

Just beyond the stretch of the woods, the lake shimmered obliviously, lapping quietly at its rocky shores. Virtually nothing remained of the dock except a few splintered planks and the steps leading down from the shore. The day passed by over the lake's mirrored surface, growing pale, and then drifting toward sunset. The police left; silence descended. Finally, the sun dipped below the horizon, leaving the lake glowing dull red in the twilight.

A shape rose out of the center of the lake. It looked a little like Petra's mother, a little like another woman. She had reddish hair and eyes so dark they were nearly black. The voice in the back room of Petra's mind had been right after all: she hadn't been able to deny the destiny that had been laid before her; she had only changed the circumstances. And with that change, the nature of the bargain had also changed.

Slowly, calmly, the wraith began to cross the lake, walking easily over the reddening waves. The figure wasn't even wet. When she reached the shore, where the dock had been, where the broken steps led up toward the deepening gloom of the sky, she stopped and looked.

The Lady of the Lake smiled.

*The end*

G. Norman Lippert has been writing for over a decade, but only began sharing his work with the world when he completed his first fan-fiction novel, *James Potter and the Hall of Elders' Crossing*. Garnering a rather shocking worldwide following, JPHEC became the topic of international media, including the Scotsman newspaper, Fox affiliates across the United States, and Canadian Public radio. Since its initial release, the story has been translated into at least five languages. Together with its sequel, *James Potter and the Curse of the Gatekeeper*, the James Potter fan-fiction series has been viewed by well over a million readers worldwide.

*The Girl on the Dock* is George's second original (non fan-fiction) story released for publication. The first story, *Flyover Country*, is available in hardcover and electronic download via lulu.com.

For more information about G. Norman Lippert and his works, visit www.elderscrossing.com or www.gatekeeperscurse.com

Keep up with news on Petra Morganstern sequels, conjecture and conversations by visiting www.girlonthedock.com

1-14

DISCARD

CPSIA information can be obtained at www.ICGtesting.com
Printed in the USA
LVOW05s1507140114

369388LV00009BA/164/P